Maquillage

THE MANY FACES OF Sally

BY STELLA STARR

authorHOUSE®

AuthorHouse™
1663 Liberty Drive
Bloomington, IN 47403
www.authorhouse.com
Phone: 1-800-839-8640

Published by AuthorHouse 3/7/2013

ISBN: 978-1-4817-0822-7 (sc)
ISBN: 978-1-4817-0823-4 (e)

SHE RACED ACROSS THE STREET dodging cars and trucks, eliciting curses from the drivers and not a few whistles. Sally was unaware of anything that did not have to do with making sure that she caught that taxi that had stopped for a red light. Breathlessly she tore open the door only to be faced by the most intense blue eyes that she had ever seen.

"I beg your pardon, madame, this taxi is taken."

"But I saw it first! I signaled to him and he stopped for me. I practically got killed running across the street. So will you please leave, I'm late for an appointment, and you're making me later."

Her long red hair was soaked and the damp tendrils framed an oval face with deep brown eyes shaded by long black lashes. Those eyes at the moment were flashing with indignation, as she realized that this man was causing her a problem. Impatiently she flipped her hair behind her shoulder and sat down on the seat. Ignoring the passenger in the back seat, she said,

"Driver, 59th and Lex please."

"Sorry, Miss, the other guy was here first."

"But you stopped for me, I signaled you."

"So did he and he got here first. That's the way I run my cab. First come first served."

"That's not fair! I'm late."

"Lady, them's the rules.

Brian Lassiter, although not particularly interested in the young girl who was so resentfully sharing the rear seat with him, and unwilling to waste more time arguing about the situation, said,

"Since we are both going to the same place perhaps we can solve this problem by sharing the cab. 9th and Lex is fine for me as well. Do you mind?

"That's fine. I don't care how we do this, I've just got to get there on time. I'll split the fare with you."

She sat at the far end of the seat while staring straight ahead. She had never shared a cab before, but just as she had thrown caution to the winds dodging traffic to secure it just so she would have ridden a camel if it had gotten her there on time. This was her first interview for a management training program and the only store that had offered her an interview.

Brian had an opportunity to observe this impatient young woman. Her hair was a mess, wet and bedraggled, she looked like a drowned kitten, however, he was able to see a perfectly shaped nose, generous lips with just a touch of lipstick and absolutely no other make-up. Her mouth was tightly set and she was obviously concerned about being on time. The thin summer dress did little to hide a well-proportioned slim figure. She caught a glimpse of herself in the cabbie's mirror, and inadvertently gasped. Digging into her large purse she pulled out a comb. Tugging ineffectually through her long auburn tresses, she succeeded in doing little except sprinkling her partner.

"Do you mind, you're getting me wet."

"Sorry, but I've got to comb my hair."

"Ladies don't comb their hair in public."

"This is not public and if you remember, it was my taxi."

She flounced around and continued to comb her hair and then took out four huge hairpins. Using the cabbie's mirror for her reflection, she succeeded in pulling her hair back into a somewhat more acceptable chignon, and proceeded to skewer it to her scalp.

"Doesn't it hurt?"

"Hurt? What do you mean?"

"Those spikes that you just stabbed yourself with, doesn't it hurt when you do that?"

She smiled, and her eyes twinkled.

"No more than the noose you tie around your neck every morning."

Inadvertently he fingered his tie.

"You're probably right," he murmured, unable now to look away from the transformed girl. He was able to see her face as the new hair style exposed creamy skin punctuated by velvety brown eyes. Her smile was delightful although brief, as she rapidly took on her earlier worried expression.

She attacked her purse again after peering over at the taximeter. Digging out two bills she proffered them to him and said,

"This should cover the fare and include a tip too."

She had already opened the door before he could refuse. He watched her as she ran up the street to the entrance of the store. Has a nice figure if she only would wear the right clothes. That dress is absolutely wrong for her, even the color isn't good. Very pretty hair. Wonder what she would look like if she were dressed properly. He then read the meter and looking at the bills in his hand realized that she had given him much too much money. One of the bills was a five. He looked up the street only to see her disappear into a revolving door.

He rushed to the entrance, but was unable to push through the crowds fast enough. By the time he got inside the department store there was no sign of her at all. He wondered where she was going in such a hurry. Probably has a date. Surprisingly, the thought of her meeting a man did not please him at all. With a practiced eye he surveyed the whole floor, noticing the traffic patterns and the displays.

It was not for nothing that he had become the most successful retailer in the business. It was his habit to travel through the country, visiting the best stores in every city, comparing and adopting new ideas, constantly updating, never content to sit back and let his past success carry him. He was one of the few department store heads who had not yet sold out to a conglomerate. He had pride in his store and his employees and even greater pride in himself. He did what he did well and expected everyone else to conform to his standards. He was a demanding employer, yet he was very fair. his salary scale was as good or better than his competitors. However, he drove himself hard and expected his executives to do the same. He chose to visit first-hand, and not to rely on reports of any one else.

His grandfather, when he had come from England in the last century, had started the store. He had been a bright, aggressive and driven man, and the store had grown as the city had grown. Each new generation had improved and gone further than the preceding one. Lassiter was now very rich. He could afford to retire or sell out. There were constant offers to do just that, but he had always refused them all. The store was his life, his only real interest and his only source of pleasure.

Sally plunged into the crowd. Impatiently she waited for the elevator to arrive. Quickly she glanced into the mirror that framed the door. This hair, it will be the death of me. I can't ever keep it neat. She turned to the side to see the effect of her hastily done coiffure. Not bad, considering the handicap, she thought. Inadvertently she smiled as she thought of that stuffy fellow passenger. "Ladies don't comb their hair in public" she mimicked him in her mind. As she did so, she remembered the depths of those piercing blue eyes. It was just a passing thought, as she recalled the real reason for her being here. After the doors opened she pressed the button marked "Administration," and tried to look as dignified as she possibly could. I'll be right on time, in spite of everything.

Her heart sank as she approached the handsome woman seated behind the receptionist's desk. About 35, her hair was cut very short in the latest mode. Large black eyes were emphasized by dark eyeliner and black mascara. True to the current vogue her cheeks were expertly rouged all the way to her temples and her lips were perfectly outlined and colored in a subtle shade of red. A white blouse with a flattering ruffled collar framed her handsome face. Sally felt quite out of style and dowdy as she approached this attractive woman..

"May I help you," she drawled?

"Yes, I have an appointment for the management training program."

She handed her the letter that she had received offering her an interview. She felt the woman's eyes sweep over her and flushed as she realized that she was being subjected to the first part of the interview. Instinctively she squared her shoulders and lifted her chin. The secretary arched her eyebrow in approval. Did this young woman have the kind of class that they were looking for in the Training Program? She appeared a little rough around the edges in that her clothes and her hair were not as smart as they should be. She rang for the young vice-president in charge of hiring for the program. To Sally she said,

"It's the first door on the left. Mr. Rawls is expecting you."

She knocked at the door indicated and was welcomed by a friendly young man seated behind the desk. He rose rapidly and came toward the door, his arm extended.

"How do you do. I'm Hank Rawls, delighted to meet you."

A tall broad-shouldered fellow, he was casually dressed In a brown tweed jacket with suede patches on the elbows, brown slacks and a regimental stripe tie. His smile and the warmth of his strong handshake did as it was intended to do. It put Sally completely at ease. The touch of anxiety that had been with her since she left the house this morning, realizing that this was the big day, dissolved unobtrusively.

"Sit down, sit down."

His first impression of this young woman was a marvelous smile, which created a double dimple on her right cheek. Her lustrous brown eyes reminded him of the center of a black-eyed Susan, while her creamy skin looked as though it would be as soft as rose petals. Even though the plain beige shirtwaist dress was not fashionable, it couldn't hide the lovely curves of her slim figure. The cloudy day had turned the office into a somber room, but her presence seemed to brighten it.

"Bit of bad weather today. You seem to have been caught in the rain."

"I'm afraid that I didn't think ahead enough. It looked as though it would just be a cloudy day, but then it began pouring."

She ruefully and ineffectually pushed back the stray tendrils that framed her face.

"I must say for someone who was obviously caught in a downpour you look remarkably good."

"Thank you."

She sat back in her chair, more and more relaxed by his friendly manner.

"I'd like to hear something about you. The bare facts of your application don't really tell me enough."

He picked up the form she had filled out and mailed in three weeks ago.

"You graduated from college last June I see. What was your major?"

"I studied psychology primarily. I wasn't sure exactly what I wanted to do, but thought that that could be the beginning of any career."

"You wanted to know what makes men tick?"

"And women, too."

"I was using 'men' in the general sense; perhaps I should have said 'people' to be current."

"That's O.K. I'm not sure that I really like a lot of the new terms. I mean 'chair-person' is a bit awkward." She grinned.

"I know what you mean. A good thing can be carried a bit too far."

"I agree. What do you think of 'personhole cover' instead of manhole cover?" she said.

"Right. How about 'penpersonship'?" She began to giggle, and he to laugh aloud.

"Or, how about 'personkind'?"

"Or 'chessperson'?"

"Or 'henchperson'?"

"Stop, oh please stop," she cried, trying to catch her breath. "It's not fair at all. I'm supposed to be making a good impression on you, and you are seeing me at my silliest. I am supposed to be a serious grown up person, excuse me, female, who is very capable, quick to learn, efficient."

He interrupted

"Loyal."

"Clean."

She dissolved again into deep rich laughter, covering her mouth and holding on to her stomach.

"Oh please stop. I hurt from laughing."

"And reverent."

Sorry, I just had to finish the Boy Scout oath.

She couldn't resist, "person scout, you mean."

At that she put her head in her hands and tears of laughter streamed down her face. Since she wore no make-up there was nothing to smear, indeed the tears served to magnify her large eyes and make them shine even more.

"It is quite apparent to me," said Hank Rawls, "that your kind of humor is needed in this organization. It is a little too staid sometimes but, the facts, madame, I need the facts. Let's make believe that we are grownups and see if we can't handle this interview properly. Now, let us start at the beginning."

"Right, sir. I will. I must control myself."

She took a deep breath. "I was born in New York City 23 years ago. I have one brother who is older than I. I went to a State college in Upper New York, and I haven't seen much of anyplace else."

"I see that your grades were very good."

"Contrary to the evidence presented today, I really am a hard worker and I do want this job," she said soberly.

"Let's continue."

"My parents both died when my brother and I were quite young and we were raised by my Aunt Helen. We were left enough money to finish college and support us up to that time. My brother is married. I like them and they like me and we have no family conflicts. As a matter of fact I introduced my brother to his wife. She is the sister of a classmate of mine. I really am very uncomplicated."

"No hidden mysteries in your family?"

"No, nothing at all interesting. Everything average. We were all quite normal. Rather pedestrian, and probably quite boring."

"And where do you live now?"

"Well, Aunt Helen is still in the City and I still have my room in her apartment, but she really wants to move somewhere in the warmer. She says that the winters are getting harder and harder for her, so as soon as I get a job, and put together a little money, I'll look for an apartment."

"Are you engaged or planning to marry soon?"

"No, not at all. I am totally free, and would like to work and establish a career.

"Don't you think that you would like to marry?"

"Of course, some day. But I really would like to be on my own for a while. I don't want the commitment of marriage for quite a long time. Because when I do marry, I want it to be right and forever so I want to take my time. I am certainly not ready now for such a commitment, and I don't think I will be for quite sometime."

"All of that is important to us at the store. I really am not being overly personal. You see, this training program is quite costly to us. It really is an education for you, you will have to work as hard or harder than you did at college, and you will not be productive for a long time. So we want to hire only people who will stay with us, at least long enough to pay off our investment in them."

He got up indicating that the interview was over. She, too, got out of the chair.

"You will hear from us very soon. I want to see two or three other applicants, but I'd like to tell you that I think you have a very good chance."

He held the door open, allowed her to precede him into the hall, walked her to the elevator and pressed the button. He gave her his hand and a very warm smile.

"I don't think I have ever enjoyed an interview so much as yours," he whispered as the elevator doors slid open. "

7

He walked back to the secretary's desk.

"What on earth was going on in your office? I never heard such a racket. Were you tickling her? I wasn't the only one who heard all of the noise either. Lassiter was up here today and he stared pretty hard at your closed door each time he went by. It looked as though it was taking a lot of control on his part not to go into the office. I never saw you so loose with a candidate before. What went on?"

"I'll tell you, she's pretty special."

"In what way? She's pretty enough, but pretty girls are a dime a dozen around here."

"I don't know what it is exactly. But there's something different about her. For one thing, she's smart."

"So are all of the rest of them."

"No, I don't mean just smart as in good grades smart, it's more than that. She's quick on the uptake, you know what I mean, and she's got a good sense of humor. She knows how to laugh at herself."

"Yeah, she sure does laugh. I heard it all the way out here. And as I said, so did Lassiter."

"It wouldn't hurt him to learn to laugh a bit. He is old sobersides himself. When's my next appointment, Mary?"

"She should be here pretty soon. I'll send her in as soon as she comes. I liked her too, what was her name?"

"Sarah, Sarah Harte. Harte! It's right too."

"Hank what's got into you? You are supposed to be impartial. I think that you've fallen for her."

"Come on, don't be silly. She's just a nice girl, pretty, stunning figure, sense of humor, bright, just your everyday average young, chick. See 'em all the time."

"So who's laughing now? You have fallen for her!"

"Never. I'm a professional to the core. Never get involved on the job. It's my motto."

He gave a mock salute.

"The only woman I have ever loved baby, is you, Mary," he kidded her.

"I will be true forever," he backed away toward his office, "and ever, and ever.... Oh! Excuse me sir."

He had backed right into Brian Lassiter.

"Hank. I'd like to see you. May I join you in your office?"

"Certainly, sir. Please come in." Hank stepped aside and let Brian enter first.

"I must say," he said "that a certain amount of decorum is expected here. There was an inordinate amount of laughter coming from this office a while ago. I really would expect more of you."

He sat down at the desk while Hank stood opposite him.

"I don't think that I have to tell you how important this training program is to me. This is one of the few stores left that is willing to invest in the future in the way that we are. But there is no point in it if we don't find the very best people. I can't quite imagine what kind of impression you must have given that last young lady."

"She was so tense at the beginning of the interview I just tried to ease the situation by making light of a few things, and she happens to have a wonderful sense of humor, and she laughs easily."

"She certainly does. I wonder if she is the right kind of a person for the job. I rather doubt it."

"Forgive me, sir, but I think you are being unfair. I, of course, haven't seen all of the candidates yet. There are two more scheduled for this afternoon, but I think that she deserves consideration."

"Good-by Hank, set a little better example, will you please?" Brian abruptly left.

Sally floated down along with the elevator. What a nice fellow that Mr. Rawls was. I hope, hope, hope, hope that I get this job. It's not that it's the only game in town, but I'd love to work with him. Good-looking, funny, pleasant. She gave a little skip as the doors opened onto the lunch room floor. Everything seems to be just right. I'm pretty sure that he liked me. He is funny."

"One please," she said aloud to the hostess.

"Follow me." She showed her to a table for two overlooking Fifth Avenue.

"Enjoy your lunch," she said as she handed her a menu. "Would you like a cocktail?"

"No, thank you, just lunch."

After looking at the menu she decided on the tuna fish salad and a glass of iced tea. Staring out the window she watched the little antlike people scurry by. They all seemed to be in a hurry, doing important things. I'm going to be part of this. I just know it. At least I hope so. He's got to see other people, but he said he enjoyed the interview. I wonder if I was too silly, I couldn't help it. He was just as silly as I. He's nice. Oh, well, I'll just hope for the best. Oh, I really want this so badly. Alternately her feelings were up and down, positive and negative about the success of the interview. I refuse to think about it any more. I'm going to go for a walk. I don't care if I get wet, I'm a mess now. I think that I'll go to the zoo. I don't care if it rains.

As she turned to see if the waitress were bringing her order, her eyes were drawn toward a tall swarthy man with magnificent blue eyes fringed with ebony lashes. His glance locked with hers as she realized that this was the man with whom she had shared the taxi this morning, but it seemed so long ago. She felt so happy and relaxed after her hopeful interview that she gave him a brilliant smile.

"You seem to be in a better mood than you were earlier. I hope that you weren't late for your appointment, wherever it was," he said. "Incidentally, I owe you money. You gave me too much for the fare this morning.

"Did I really?" She dug into her huge purse again, and came up with her wallet. "How much extra did I give you?" She put it away suddenly. "I really don't care. I think my appointment was successful and I would have had to pay for the whole fare anyway if you hadn't usurped my taxi, so please be my guest," she said expansively.

"I won't hear of it. Please allow me to pay you back."

"No way. This has got to be my lucky day. Please let it go."

"I don't feel right about it."

"You have to. It was a lucky omen." She smiled brilliantly, and turned to finish her lunch.

Unused to being dismissed by anyone, and even more unused to having his offers rejected, he moved through the lunchroom uncomfortably, yet intrigued by her self-possession. Brian was a man who had no lack of female companionship. As a matter of fact he was a much sought after bachelor. Involved as he was in his business he had never really had the time to pay the necessary attention to any woman in order to develop a good and lasting relationship. A good deal of his interest in the business had been due, in fact, to a deliberate effort on his part. He wanted it to be his life and it was. He kept his relationships quite casual. There were plenty of women who would have liked to become Mrs. Lassiter, not only for the social prestige and wealth that it would bring, but also because he was such an attractive man. That he was emotionally elusive only seemed to add to his charm. It was not a ploy, however, he wanted it that way.

This girl, however, was a puzzle. She was such a pretty thing and yet she was the first woman he had met who seemed unaware, indeed unconcerned, about her beauty. The memory of her hasty toilette in the taxi amused him. He knew of no other girl who would have gotten herself prepared for what was obviously an important meeting with such little fuss. He realized how relieved he had been to see her sitting there obviously unaccompanied. So she had not had a date after all. It was not another man.

Sally had gone to the zoo after lunch and thought about her day. As amused as she had been by the seals and the chimpanzees, she found that she kept drifting back to the tall man with the intense blue eyes. As a matter of fact, she had met two interesting men in one day.

It never rains but it pours. I liked Mr. Rawls. He was so friendly and nice. I think he liked me too, but I guess it depends on the competition. He has to give everyone a fair chance. And then she thought again about the man with whom she had shared the cab. There was a kind of magnetism about him. I really didn't like him very much. He was kind of cold in the cab, very proper, doesn't look as though he'd be much fun. I wonder how old he is. That little touch of gray at the temples is very attractive, and the contrast of his eyes and black hair. Unbidden the thought came, is he married? What has that to do with me anyway? I don't even know who he is nor do I really care. I have a job to look forward to and by golly, I sure hope I get it. Otherwise I'm not sure just what I'll do.

Mary had watched Sally with interest as she waited for Hank to see her. Hank really seemed to have liked her. It was not like him. He was generally such an industrious, serious man, who was obviously trying to reach the top of the organization. He and Lassiter had an understanding that Hank was being groomed for the second position. She was surprised to see his loss of control with Sally. Not that he had done anything wrong. Not at all. But Lassiter sure had dressed him down, and surprisingly Hank had not been particularly chagrined. That girl must have something, I guess. Mary knew that Sally would have two strikes against her when Lassiter found out that she had been the source of merriment that day. She felt protective of Hank, and hoped that he would have his way in hiring Sally. He needs some fun in his life. If he kept up the intensity of his devotion to the job, he would end up a bachelor like Lassiter.

Mary looked her usual elegant self in a gray man-tailored flannel suit. Again, her face was framed by a ruffled collar but this time it was in gray silk. A good-looking woman, she had worked for Lassiter's since she had graduated from college herself, and for many years had been in love with Brian. Lassiter was very fond of Mary. She was the only exception to his rule of never mixing his business with his personal life. They had spent some vacations together, and occasionally had dinner and the night. But Brian had made it very clear from the beginning that there was no way in the world that there could be more than this casual relationship. His marriage was to the store. By now Mary had accepted it. She knew that she could never have him and was willing to take what little that he was willing to share with her. She had resigned herself and kept herself and her comfortable apartment ready for the times that Brian cared to use them. Her one solace was that he had no closer a relationship with any else. She had more of him that any other woman and with that she had to be content.

Sally was remarkably at ease as she waited for Hank to call her in for her second interview. She knew that he had liked her, and she felt confident today. She was dressed very simply in a blue blazer with a blue plaid kilt carefully pinned so that there was not too much exposure of her more than shapely leg. It was matched with a beige turtleneck pullover and she had carefully pulled her recalcitrant locks into a bun; only a very few wisps escaped the tight knot. Actually, the softness around her face was flattering. She had chosen an antique bar pin of small pearls that had been her mother's to adorn her lapel. She was understated and very handsome. Again she wore very little make-up, just a touch of lipstick. Her natural coloring brought a light blush to her cheeks. As usual she had not paid more than the minimum necessary to her toilette. Her concern was only that of being hired and it never occurred to her that it would be done for any other reason than her competency.

"You can go in now, Miss Harte," said Mary. As she arose Hank came into the reception area to meet her. He offered his hand.

"I'm very glad to see you again. Won't you come in, please. The committee has decided to offer you the job on probation. You are, of course, if you are willing, to be a roving salesgirl through the store. It is not really the easiest thing in the world, but our policy is to expose our trainees to the whole operation. It is difficult because you really don't have enough time to become acquainted with the stock and the buyers or fellow sales personnel. You will be spending about a week in each department and after that period is over, you will be evaluated by the manager in each department as well as by Mr. Lassiter and me. This will be your probationary period. After you have been approved by all of those who are going to judge you, you will be selected to work with the buyer in one of the departments. That really is as far as we can go now in discussing it because after that period is over, each candidate has a program tailored to his or her needs and those of the store. I hope that this can be the beginning of a long and mutually rewarding relationship."

Sally, her eyes wide and her mouth frozen into a grin, was afraid to take a breath. She was afraid that she would wake up and that it was a dream. She hadn't expected such a positive definite answer so quickly.

"Do I accept, of course I do. I can't wait to begin."

"You know, the salary is very small. As I told you, at the beginning our trainees cost us more than they are able to produce."

"When can I start Mr. Rawls?"

She was determined to be more formal than she had been the last time. She wanted to make sure that he and she would have a solid professional relationship.

"We will start you literally on the ground floor. You will be working at the cosmetics counter. I'll take you down now and introduce you to Joan, the manager of the department, and she can fill you in on all of the details. How she wants you to dress, what make-up, etc."

She stood up and walked over to his desk.

"Thank you so very much. I appreciate the opportunity to prove myself. I will work very hard."

She offered her hand to him. For Sally, it was simply a gesture of respect and gratitude. However, for Hank, it was more than that. The touch of her hand was exciting. He felt a current leap to his. At least he thought that he did, but looking at her serene face he realized that it was all wishing on his part. It was true, he had fallen for her. It was equally true that she saw him as nothing more than a pleasant employer.

She couldn't wait to call Aunt Helen.

"I got it! I got it! No, it doesn't pay very much. In fact, it really is slave wages, but I figure it's like tuition for me. I'm learning a trade. And now, Aunt Helen, as soon as probation is over, I look for an apartment. I'll see you at dinner, I just couldn't wait to tell you. No, I want to walk through the park and then I think I'll go to the

Museum. They have a wonderful exhibit about different kinds of Pyramids, Mexican, Egyptian and I don't know, who ever else built them. I'm so happy. Good-by. See you later."

She whirled of around and collided with a tall man. Her purse flew to the floor. As she and he bent together to pick it up, they knocked heads and its contents spilled all over the floor.

"You are an impetuous little person, aren't you! For heaven's sake, it is my taxi companion."

"Are you here again? You certainly must like shopping," she said. "You must be Lassiter's best customer."

"Yes, I come here quite often," he smiled. "It looks as though you are in your usual rush to get somewhere."

"Oh, it's just such a beautiful day I want to go into the park for a long walk. And then to the museum."

She looked up at him. Electricity flashed from his eyes. He was seeing right into her soul! He handed her the purse and as their hands accidentally touched, she felt as though she were stung. There was something in his touch that frightened her. She searched his face to see if he had felt the spark too. It was then she realized that he was holding her hand.

"Thank you." She abruptly pulled away from him. "Thank you very much. I must collect all of my things."

"Let me help you, here you are."

She found herself blushing and with every touch of his hand as he handed her lipstick, pencils, date book, checkbook and her wallet, all of which she stuffed into her purse without looking at them, as she found herself more and more shaken.

"Thank you again."

He took her elbow and lifted her to her feet. While staring into her face,

"You are so lovely," he murmured "You are a really beautiful girl. May I walk with you in the park."

"What do you mean?" she stammered, so thrown by his nearness.

"Walk - with you - in the park - may I join you?"

Feeling as though she had no control over her mind or body, dazedly she whispered,

"Yes, of course, of course."

Together they walked silently down the few blocks to the park and as one turned into the entrance. Apparently he had been unnerved as she by the encounter. There seemed no need for words, just the other's presence was enough. Silently he took her hand. She, glancing shyly up at him, saw his gaze fastened on her face. At last he said,

"My name is Brian, what is yours?"

"Sally, my name is Sally."

"I liked your hair better when it poured down your back. You looked less serious."

"You certainly seem to be serious, as a matter of fact, you look as though you just lost your last friend." Turning to face him and staring into his eyes she said, "I am probably crazy, but I think that I have just found my best friend."

He took her in his arms, saying,

"If you are crazy, I am too, because I know that I have just found something and someone that I didn't even know I was looking for."

He bent down then and, holding her tightly, lowered his lips to hers. They stood just that way for what seemed to Sally an eternity. She felt as though she really was suspended in time, as she became aware of portions of her body that she had not known even known existed. The kiss was the deepest that she had ever had. Sally was lost.

Abruptly she pulled away, and said,

"What must you think of me. I don't even know you. I have never done that before, I never felt that way before. I am absolutely mortified."

She turned and ran toward the park entrance, hairpins falling out as she ran, her long red hair cascading down her back.

Brian ran after her but she had crossed the bridle path just as New York's Mounted Police were exercising their horses. He was caught. Frustrated he watched as she rounded the curve of the path. Impatiently, he waited as the never-ending line of horses walked slowly by. By the time he was able to cross, she had completely disappeared. Cursing his luck he ran down the path after her, hoping that she would retrace their steps, but to no avail. It was as though she had been swallowed into a labyrinth. Disconsolately, he slowed his pace and tried to take stock of the situation. Up until a short time ago he had been a happy man. He had organized his life as he wanted it. He was pleased with his relationship with Mary and the other casual relationships that he enjoyed. Suddenly, he had been faced with the fact that there was a woman with whom he might like to share a life. Her innocent reciprocation of what he realized might be a deep passion only endeared her to him further. It was her very innocence that he prized. Her beauty was obvious, but there were many who had that asset; it was her naiveté spiced by her independence that attracted him. I met her twice, no three times in this general area. Perhaps it isn't too much to hope that she will come again to the store. I think that I will make myself more in evidence. I'll spend more time observing the functioning of the first floor.

Sally ran all the way out of the park. She was horrified at her behavior. Why, I know nothing about him. He could be married, engaged, a murderer, anything, but he is not suitable for me. First, I don't want to be involved with anyone, not anyone, emotionally at this point in my life; secondly, I can't imagine responding the way that I did. It is so unlike me. What could have happened? The memory of that kiss returned and she shivered with the pleasure of it. I hate this feeling of being out of control. I hope that I never,never see him again. But the thought of there being no repetition of the moment was even more painful than her humiliation at what she had said and done. A complete stranger, I actually told him that I've been looking for him all of my life. I can't believe that I said that. I can't believe that I kissed him in that way, either. She excoriated herself for her behavior and then reveled in the feeling of utter bliss alternating with torment that she might never see him again.

AUNT HELEN GREETED HER AT the door.

"Tell me everything honey. I can't wait to hear it. She followed Sally into the brightly lit living room and caught a glimpse of her unhappy face.

"Why, honey, what's wrong? You sounded so happy on the phone. You were bubbling all over and now you look as though you lost your best friend."

"It's nothing, Aunt Helen I think that I'm just over-excited and a little fearful as to whether I can do the job. It's going to be hard work."

"Well, of course, it is. But any interesting job is going to be hard. If it were easy, you would be bored silly in one week. No, knowing you I would say you would last only one day. You know, at your graduation, I don't know if I ever told you, the Dean told me that there was absolutely no job that he wouldn't recommend you for. He said that you were one of the best students that had ever attended that school, and with your looks and persistence, there was nothing to stop you from reaching the top.

" Of course your work has to be challenging and," she added more gently, "you're scared. I would hope that you wouldn't approach a new job in a cocky fashion. You have always had a realistic but at the same time somewhat humble view of yourself." She put her arm around Sally's shoulder. The thing to do now is to take a long hot bath, relax and I'll make you a light supper."

Sally smiled in affection at this loving lady, who had always adored and cared for her since she was such a young child. There was nothing that Aunt Helen couldn't fix by a long hot bath. It was her prescription for every ill in the world. If it were only nerves about the job, Sally was sure that the bath would do the trick. But what do you do when you realize that you have fallen in love with a man you know nothing about, are sure you will never see again and worst of all with whom you are convinced that you made an utter fool of yourself?

She went into the bathroom and turned on the hot taps. I'll give it a try. She poured bath oil into the tub. It released its odor as it was diluted in the hot water and enveloped Sally in a swirl of sensuous scent. Far from removing the cause of her unhappiness, the aroma triggered a wave of longing. She wished that she were in his arms again. She stepped into the tub and gave herself up into a world of daydreams.

Brian was waiting for Hank Rawls to report to him. He sat on the terrace of his apartment. After many years of living in an overlarge, dark duplex on Park Avenue, he had decided to build the home of his dreams overlooking Central Park where he could have an ever changing view. He had spared no expense. In true Lassiter fashion, he had hired the best architect available and then proceeded to tell him exactly how to do his job. He went through three of them before he was finally able to work comfortably with any. Brian was a brilliant, as well as a stubborn, man. He had done a great deal of research on the problems of building on top of a completed structure. He really wanted an architect to simply implement his own ideas. Among them were a swimming pool, sauna, exercise rooms and a special terrace. After the apartment had been completed to his satisfaction, he then proceeded to decorate it by himself. He sketched everything that he wanted and then tossed the ideas to the City's most renowned decorator. She, of course, had no say, her suggestions were ignored, all she was able to do was to buy what he wanted. When it finally was finished he was very pleased. It even surpassed his expectations and, of course, it really was his own creation.

In one of the store's elevator cabs above the control panel was a keyhole. That was the only way to reach the apartment. Only Brian, Hank Rawls and servants, had a key. It was an aerie, a retreat, he felt untouchable and truly the king of all he surveyed. It was as though Central Park were his domain, and he were the lord of the castle.

The elevator doors opened into a small entrance hall, and as Hank entered the apartment he was again impressed by the understated excellent taste of his employer. The walls were covered with Fortuni silk and hung with exquisite Japanese prints and a magnificent sumi wash of Sesshu. Their delicacy was breathtaking. The maid answered the door and he saw again the exquisite home. A large two-story room whose back wall was filled with books floor to ceiling had two niches filled by deep comfortable leather couches which were designed for curling up with a favorite book and perhaps a glass of wine. A glass wall overlooked Central Park. Doors opened out to a broad terrace, on which was a meticulously designed miniature Japanese garden, planned so as to give the illusion that the view extended far past the confines of the terrace wall. A waterfall in the corner led to a small pond. Evergreens, rocks and irregular stepping stones were placed on a bed of sand which was raked into patterns every day. Lassiter had wanted to reproduce temple gardens such as those he had seen in Japan which are designed to produce a feeling of harmony with nature. The sound of the water and the flow of the stream were all conducive to a feeling of tranquility. Stepping stones, irregularly placed, invited use not just observation

Whenever he came into that magnificent room and walked over to the view of the balcony, he too felt as though his cares were lifted.

His employer was sitting with a Martini while gazing at the garden. Even it had been unable to work its charm for him that evening. He was troubled by his encounter with that girl about whom he knew nothing except her first name.

"How did your day go," he asked as he realized that Hank was standing there. "Did you order a drink?"

"Yes, thanks, I already have it and my day went just fine. I think that the advertisement program that we planned is pretty good, but I have something new that I would like to try. You know that somehow or other most of the women who work for the store are good-looking, at least they are quite passable."

"Uh huh, I wonder how that has happened, Hank."

"Now wait, I don't say that I hire only on that basis, but I admit that it can be a minor factor. After all our business is sales, and most people like to buy from pretty people, right?"

"Right, so what is your point."

"I think that we should use them."

"We do, they are sales people."

"No, I mean, this is the decade of the 'ordinary' people, not models from some agency, they are really real. Their sincerity practically comes out and grabs you by the throat."

"That's all true," said Brian glad to be involved in a discussion other than that of the elusive Sally. "Go on."

"Well, my idea is that we should have our real sales personnel do our advertising for us instead of some anonymous model who doesn't look like anyone at all."

"But models are designed to be different. If they looked like normal people, they wouldn't photograph well and show off the clothes to advantage, they have to be size 3 or some ridiculous number like that."

"Right, that's all true, but I think that the public is getting away from that idea. They would like to see how clothes really look on normal women. Anyway, let me go on." He took a drag on his cigarette. "I'd like to do something experimental. Why can't we use some of our own people to show our clothes for our ads. We could have them posing in the store, or in the park, or even in front of the Japanese garden."

"You know I hate to have my retreat become a part of the store. I haven't ever invited more than three or four people up here."

"OK, that doesn't have to be done, but what about the idea. What do you think?"

"I think that it has possibilities. As a matter of fact I think it's good. Very good."

After Hank left, Brian sat for many hours gazing out onto the garden suspended in thought. He kept imagining Sally in his garden. His dream was so real he felt he could walk over and touch her.

Sally arrived for work the next morning confident that she would lose herself in the excitement of the new job. She tried very hard to concentrate, yet found that she kept looking around for that man whom she could not get out of her mind. Twice, no three times he had been in this general vicinity. Was it illogical to think that he would appear again? She did not want to see him again. That was her conscious thought. And yet, every time she saw a tall dark man going past the cosmetics counter, her heart flipped. This is impossible, she thought, I can't continue this way.

She approached a poorly dressed older woman, who was certainly not up to the Fifth Avenue standards of most of the store's customers and found her handling a jar of turtle oil cream.

"How much is this, Miss?" Her work-worn hands fondled the pretty package.

"Ah, good morning, Madam, and how are you today." She answered in her new selling voice. "It sells for $44 a jar, plus tax."

"That sure is a lot, but it's supposed to make your skin so young."

"Yes, it's supposed to, but I agree with you that's a lot of money."

She looked at the withered cheeks, and thought to herself how unfair it was that this poor woman had been sold a bill of goods by some advertising firm. That $44 could be used to much better advantage. She found that there was no way that she could go along with the fictionthat the "Turtle Oil" in the creme would make her even a day younger. She leaned toward the tired looking woman.

"If you want a good lubricant for your skin, you'd do much better to go to the drugstore and buy their cheapest cold cream. There's no reason for you to pay for all of that Madison Avenue advertising. Did you ever see a turtle's skin? I wouldn't want mine to look like that." She solemnly winked at the woman whose eyes filled with tears.

"I never met a salesgirl like you. Thankyou, thankyou."

She turned and slowly walked out of the store.

The manager who had observed the conversation, but fortunately had not overheard Sally's part, came over. "I guess you couldn't make the sale. Don't worry, she was just window shopping. She's not our kind. You'll get the next one."

Sally looked at her without speaking. Is this what this business is? Selling valueless products to people who can't afford them? I'm not so sure that's what I want to do. She took a deep breath, and decided that she wouldn't let that incident color her day. There will be other legitimate sales. People do like to look pretty, and make-up does, I suppose, make them feel better about themselves, and so I guess it's OK. But she hadn't really convinced herself, and she began to have some doubts about her chosen profession.

"Incidentally," she heard the manager say, "I think that you ought to wear a little more make-up. It always pays to look as though you believe in the product you're selling."

Sally looked at Joan's carefully applied makeup and thought to herself, I don't even know what that woman really looks like. Her eyeshadow is so dark, her mouth so red, and her rouge covers so much of her face, I don't know where she ends and the make-up begins.

She knew that this department was not going to be where she wanted to spend time. She also knew that there were going to be areas that she enjoyed and areas that she didn't, so she decided to say nothing except, "Do you think so?" and did nothing about it. Joan Darcy, however, would remember when it came time to make a report on Sally. The report would mention something about an uncooperative attitude.

At her lunch break she hurried upstairs to the small tea-room where she had eaten the other day. She half-hoped and-half feared that she would see Brian again. After ordering she sat staring out at the park below. She had slipped out of her shoes and was rubbing one sore foot on the other, grateful for the discomfort, as it took her mind from the memories of yesterday.

"May I join you?"

She looked up into the smiling face of Hank Rawls. Delighted at this new distraction and because she genuinely liked him she answered, with a broad smile,

"Of course, I'm delighted to see you. Please do."

"Lunch-break? How's the day going?"

"Well, I don't think that I'm such a great sales person." She was tempted to tell him the story of the poor woman and remembered in time that he was her boss, and her job was to make sales.

"It's tiring, at first, but when you get the hang of it it's not too bad. You know that this apprenticeship is really only to acquaint you with the store and all of its workings. Mr. Lassiter believes in working up from the bottom. I was finally able to convince him that it wasn't necessary for our executive trainees to clean the washrooms."

She giggled. Her eyes crinkled and the deep dimple sprang into being.

"He sounds like an ogre. Did he ever go through that routine himself?"

"Oh yes, he's done everything, even that. He's very demanding but he doesn't expect anything of anyone that he wouldn't do himself. I've even seen him working in the lunch room."

"When he waits on table, does he wear a frilly apron as well?"

Somehow the image of Lassiter in a frilly apron convulsed Hank. He began laughing so hard at the ridiculous imaginary spectacle, that

22

Sally found herself caught up in his hilarity. She began to laugh at his laughter. Several of the patrons turned around to see the cause of all of the noise.

Hank got out of his seat and came around to the other side of the table to give Sally a big hug. She was so grateful for his warmth and lightheartedness after her morning of discomfort that she returned the embrace, burying her face in his jacket. To Hank, her action was meaningful because he was extraordinarily attracted to this lively girl. To Sally, it was simply the delight in a kindhearted man and seeming protector. He caressed her lovely hair, his hand lingering on the gentle waves.

It was at this paint that Brian Lassiter entered the tea-room. He was astounded to see Hank Rawls with his arms around a strange woman. Only after he had released her and gone back to his own seat was Brian able to see who she was. His face lost all color as he observed the seemingly tender scene. He was furious. Enraged that he had let his feelings go to such an extent that he had included Sally in his daydreams, incensed that she appeared to be doing the same thing with Hank that she had done with him, he forced himself to sit down at a table where he could see but not be seen. How could she be such a slut? Does she embrace all men she meets in the same way? Envious that another man was holding her, his thoughts roiled around until they gelled into one emotion - rage. Anger because she had in his eyes betrayed him. Betrayed his trust in her, betrayed the emotions he had invested in her, and worst of all betrayed the image of her that he had created in his own mind.

He slipped out of the room and went up to his apartment. Angrily he called the maid for a drink and then sat in front of his tranquil Japanese garden.

He was furious with Hank. This was his trusted lieutenant. In all fairness he knew that Hank had no idea that he was interested in the girl. However, he felt that his conduct was inappropriate. That's twice now I've found him lacking in judgment. Once when there was all of that hysterical laughter coming from his office, and now making an exhibition of himself. Should I fire him? No, that was too drastic. He was good, he was the best in the business, I'm lucky to have him. No, it must be her fault. She is obviously a wanton. He's too good to lose. There must be something wrong with me to get myself so involved with a girl of low morals. I have to get away.

He picked up the phone.

"Mary, let Kitty take over for you. I want to go out to the beach house. Get ready to leave. I'll pick you up. Is twenty minutes enough time? Well, how long? All right, we'll be gone until Monday. Hurry."

Mary met him at the car which he had impatiently double-parked.

"What took you so long?"

"For heaven's sake Brian, I had to get out of the office, pack, change, what's your hurry? I had to call out there and tell them we were coming."

She had not even had time to pack properly as she had recognized the royal command. Hastily she had thrown on a pair of designer jeans which clung to and emphasized all of the good portions of her anatomy. They complemented an emerald green velour top which set off her dark hair and eyes, and a darker green silk Hermes scarf around her throat. She hoped that she hadn't forgotten anything. It was not possible to easily find replacements because the beach house was on an island in the middle of the Sound. However, recognizing a black mood when she saw one, she was glad that it was always to her that he turned when he was unhappy. I ought to think of myself as an emotional Florence Nightingale. Sometimes she resented the role, but realizing her importance to him in at least this area, she was willing to accept it.

Brian drove intensely, and furiously, cutting in and out and tailgating. She had never seen such erratic and self-destructive driving.

"I hope that are not planning on committing suicide, because it would be murder as well, and I'm not quite ready to die. Slow down, for God's sake, will you! I've punched a hole in the floor trying to help you brake this careening death trap. Brian, I've never seen you like this. What's wrong?"

For an answer she received such a dark look that she said no more, but he did slow down and the rest of the trip went without incident. When they arrived at the dock, the small launch was waiting with Artie, the caretaker of the island.

"Afternoon, sir, how have you been? Glad to see you out here. It's been quite awhile. My wife opened up all of the rooms and got everything ready. I think we thought of everything you will need. I got enough provisions for a week."

"A week's enough. No problem." She shook the man's hand and Mary said, "Nice to see you again."

Artie grunted. He didn't particularly like Mary. He didn't trust women who wore all of that paint on their face. Even though they always slept in separate rooms, he didn't think that it was right that she should come along with Brian and be the only guest in the large house.

The "camp" as Brian called it was hardly that. It had been designed in the twenties by his grandfather to be used as a luxurious seaside retreat. The veranda, surrounding four sides of the house made it possible to see the sea from any place, was furnished with many old-fashioned comfortable, wicker rocking chairs. Several fans were overhead to enhance the incoming seabreezes. Inside, mirrors on most walls caught reflections of the dunes and the sea, bringing light into all the downstairs rooms. A large ballroom with a dais for musicians at one end, extended the length of the house, while on the opposite side of the hall, doors led to a large but comfortable sitting room and an immense dining room. All of the furniture was designed for comfort and was in excellent taste. Because they had to contend with the dampness of the ocean, the furnishings in spite of the magnificence of the house were light and bright, easily aired so that there was little mustiness. The kitchen was a marvel to behold. It looked like, and indeed had been used as though it were, a restaurant kitchen. A massive 8-burner stove with four ovens ruled the cavernous room. Huge double refrigerators and freezers stood ready to provide banquets for fifty or even more if need be. The dining room held a Sheraton table seating twelve when closed and there were twenty-four Queen Anne chairs covered with yellow chintz. A large glass cabinet held the Georgian silverware which had been in the family ever since the original Lassiter had purchased it in England. It had been difficult, but not impossible, to find silversmiths to double the quantity. All had enjoyed so much use over the years that it was almost impossible to distinguish the originals from the reproductions. There were silver tea and coffee service and silver serving plates. Most of it all was kept wrapped up in Pacific cloths and plastic wrap these days. Otherwise, Artie and his wife would never be able to keep up with the job of polishing. It was hardly a "camp", but a holdover from the roaring twenties.

Brian loved the isolation of the island, and loved the luxury of it all. He remembered when the house was full of visitors who came out for weeks at a time. They had created their own amusements, treasure-hunts, charades, parodies, putting on Gilbert and Sullivan operettas and any other diversions and games they could devise. There had been a great deal of fun there. But Brian had not felt like that kind of relaxation for a long time. Today he certainly didn't want anyone else but Mary around. Maybe I should sell it. It represents another era. But what would be the point. I don't need or want the money. Let it be. All of this went through his mind as he climbed the olden oak stairs. The bannister felt as though it had been carved to fit his hand alone. Every time he ascended, he marveled at the grace of the curve of the rail. The first landing had a cushioned seat under a tremendous window overlooking the sea. He had loved to curl up there and read or daydream, as he stared out into the infinite ocean, about feats of derring-do and princesses rescued from pirate ships. When he was young, some of the happiest memories of an only child were the long summer days spent here. He looked down at the dock and saw that Artie had taken the sailboat out and it was ready for him whenever he wanted it.

Although he was staring at the sea he saw again the scene of Hank with his arms around Sally. A slow black anger arose. There was pain as well, as he remembered the feel of her lissome body in his arms, the memory as elusive as the young girl herself. Impatiently he pushed back the sadness and reveled in the anger. It was Mary, who bore the brunt of his pain and fury. But she wasn't aware that she was a substitute that weekend.

"Mary, tell Hank that I want a meeting of all of the managers in my office, ASAP." Brian had decided to try to forget Hank's role in his disillusionment with Sally. He knew that Hank was an excellent executive and that he would be very hard to replace. He wouldn't allow his personal feelings to interfere with business.

The weekend away at the island had tempered his anger. He had buried it deeply and resolved not to think of her again. He had exorcised his rage and frustration. Mary had been his instrument.

He was anxious to go ahead with the suggestion that Hank had made about using the stores personnel in its advertising. He wanted to get started with it. He had even reconsidered and agreed that his apartment would be a marvelous place to pose some of the women.

He welcomed Hank into his office with anticipation. He was anxious to throw himself into this new project.

"Well, what have you done so far?"

"First of all, I had to go through all of the departments to see what their needs were and how much they were planning to spend on advertising. Second, I have to coordinate the whole thing. Now what I wanted to ask you is this, how far do we have to go in being truthful. What I mean is do you think that the lady who has been selling lingerie has to be the one who is modeling it, or do you think that we can use just any of the employees, just so long as they are our employees?"

"I think that it's up to you. If you have any scruples about mixing and matching, why can't you just put that person in temporarily on the floor?"

"Shrewd as usual, Mr. L. An excellent idea. That's real truth in advertising! Now, I just search for all of the lovelies and reassign them."

"Don't take it too far. I don't want the whole store disrupted. Why don't you just start with those who photograph well and happen to be selling something interesting."

"Right. I'm on my way. I had another thought."

"Shoot, most of yours have been pretty good lately." Brian deliberately suppressed a wave of anger as the scene in the tea-room rose unbidden.

Hank, unaware that Brian was in any way displeased with him, continued,

"What happens if we were to use some exotic places in the campaign. As a tie-in, maybe there could be a contest, best salesperson, most popular salesperson, highest sales record, most pleasant salesperson, and then the winner would go on a tour, and we get to follow her with appropriate cameras, clothes, luggage, nighties, pots, pans, mattresses, bedding....?"

"Up to a point you've got a great idea, but I can't see shipping a washing machine out to Bali so that we can have a girl pose with it on the beach."

Hank sat up. He had been lounging, sitting on the tail of his spine.

"You've got it! That would be terrific! Surrealist but certainly eye-catching."

Brian caught his enthusiasm.

"Great. We'll call it "Lassiter's, the store where all of your fantasies come true," or something to that effect."

"It could be terrific, and I just know that there's not one salesperson who won't be excited. It may end up boosting our sales for internal reasons, a little competition never hurt 'em. It's going to be fun as well as effective."

After a week when Sally had gone out on a few dates with some old boyfriends, and tried to think as little as possible about the mysterious stranger who had touched her soul so deeply, she came to work on Monday bound and determined to make a success of any area to which she was assigned. Much to Joan Darcy's surprise, she found her behind the counter applying practically every kind of make-up that the store sold. First she put on a cream base, then she used a blusher, emphasizing her high cheekbones and the dark hollows beneath.

"Joan, do you think the midnight blue shadow or the plum would be better?

Joan pleased to be asked, made several suggestions.

"Here, climb up on the stool and leave it to me."

She helped her to do her eyes and then pulled her red hair into an upsweep letting strategically placed wisps fall free. Finally, she stepped away from her handiwork

"I never expected you to look like that. I knew you were good-looking, but baby, you're breathtaking, make-up can really help even a beauty like you."

"Me? You're kidding. I know that I'm OK, nice looking, attractive even, sometimes, but a beauty, no way in the world. Here, let me take a look."

Joan had managed to create a new face by carefully emphasizing her bone structure by rouging her cheeks, plumping her mouth, enlarging her luminous eyes, using an assortment of brushes and puffs and all the other tricks of the trade. Sally was surprised at her own reflection. It was a good-looking girl all right, but it wasn't the Sally she knew. She was dismayed.

"Joan. *You* have created a good-looking woman, but that's not me."

"Well, it sure ain't me. It's on your shoulders, so it's got to be you. You look absolutely smashing."

She shrugged, "I hope that at least it helps to sell cosmetics because I really like to look like me, not someone else."

"You'll get used to it. It's impossible not to, you're stunning. Just watch. Everyone who passes the counter is looking at you. Now's the time to smile, try to catch them, and sell them something."

Joan thought to herself, I hope that she can do something about her rotten sales record of last week. I would hate to give her a bad report, she's an awfully nice girl. I hope that she does better. I'll be able to average it if she picks up her sales.

Sally got caught up in the spirit of the whole thing. She felt as though she were at a masquerade, and the person who was hidden behind the mask was obliterated by it, thereby allowing her to be anonymous. She almost felt as though the facade would take over her real personality.

"May I help you, sir?" A tall man was leaning against her counter, facing the Fifth Avenue street entrance. He turned around with a smile.

"No, thank you, I'm just waiting here. I won't stay long. Do you mind?"

It was Brian but he made no sign of recognition. Grateful, and at the same time angry and hurt at his being able to forget her so soon, when her heart had been breaking for him for five days, she quickly mumbled,

"No, not at all," and fled around the corner to the other side of the counter. I wonder why he's always around here. She approached Joan who was writing up a sale.

"Have you seen a very tall dark man with a touch of gray at the temples, he was wearing an oxford gray suit, and I didn't notice anything else. Except his eyes.

"Good looking?"

"Very."

"How old - wait a minute, let me finish this sales slip."

"Here you are ma'am thank you. I hope you enjoy the lipstick." She handed the pretty package tied with a violet ribbon to her customer. She went back to Sally.

"How old did you say he was?"

"I don't know, middle late thirties."

"Interesting looking?"

"Oh yes," she sighed. "I've seen him around here three times. I think his first name is Brian."

"Is he still here?"

"No, he's disappeared."

"Beats me, the only Brian I have ever heard of is Brian Lassiter."

"Lassiter, does he have something to do with the store?"

"Of course - he owns it."

"What does he look like?"

"I don't know. Nobody I know has ever seen him. So I couldn't tell you. I think he's a much older man, probably in his 60s or so."

At this news, Sally said,

"Joan, it's time for a lunch break." She fled out of the store, not daring to look behind.

The whole store was agog with the news of the new sales campaign. All of the salesclerks were coming to work even more carefully dressed and made up than usual. It was known that Hank was on a scouting expedition to choose those whom he thought would do well in the modeling program. Not only were they interested in participating in the store program, but they were thinking ahead to the winning of the promotion, so that they would have a chance to visit those "exotic" places that Hank had outlined in his presentation. Everyone was on their toes and the store had never run more smoothly.

"I must hand it to you Hank," said Brian. "Even if the sales campaign does nothing as far as the advertising success is concerned, the functioning of the store is incredible. In just one day since you announced the program I can see a difference in the salespeople's attitude. It was a stroke of genius."

"I don't know about that, let's see how long the momentum lasts."

"Well, accept my congratulations for today anyway."

"That I do, that I do, but now I have to get down to the really hard job. Picking out the models. Everyone looks so spiffy, it's going to be hard. The problem is that some people who are really good-looking don't necessarily photograph well. So I think that we are going to have tests made of anyone we feel is promising."

"I'm going to start on the ground floor," Hank continued. "Do you want to do it with me, or is the whole thing in my lap?"

"No, I'd rather see the photos after they are finished and then I'll help you to make the final decisions."

Hank went down to the first floor, where generally the most attractive women were placed in cosmetics, perfumes, jewelry, and lingerie. Brian had always wanted the prettiest down there because he said that they set the tone of the store. Of course, Hank had based his new program on the belief that those women thought that they themselves could look like the model.

He came over to Joan's counter.

"Well, how are you doing, Joan. What have the sales been like for the last week?"

"They could be better but Sally, I think, is going to improve this week now that she's into the swing of it."

Joan was beautifully dressed in tight-fitting black slacks with a persimmon silk shirt. She had a simple silver necklace around her throat and a matching silver bangle bracelet. Her black hair was swept up and of course her make-up was a bit obvious as usual. However, she was a handsome and eye-catching woman. She had become over the years one of the best salespeople in the store and she was pretty sure that she would be one of the lucky few.

Hank thought so too. He liked Joan as well. However, he had never stepped out of line with her as he had with Sally.

"Now," he asked, "Where is Sally?"

"She'll be back in a moment. Her break is almost over."

Hank did not recognize the young woman who was walking toward him. Her red hair was piled on top of her head casually with just a few loose curls surrounding her face. She wore a forest-green pleated skirt and a nile green turtle neck shirt, her small waist was cinched by a moss green leather belt. Her face was carefully made up with an emphasis on her eyes, causing them to appear huge and luminous. Dark green was the shade with a lighter green above the eye. Her mouth was carefully outlined and blusher used to emphasize her good bone structure.

She walked easily in a pair of high-heeled pumps. She was breath-taking.

"Hi, it's so good to see you."

She rushed forward to give him her hand. It was only then that he realized that this was the woman to whom he was so attracted.

"Sally, I did *not* recognize you. What have you done to yourself?"

Her smile wavered. "Don't you like it? Joan and I thought that the make-up would be good for business."

31

"Like it? You are unbelievably gorgeous. But it makes you so different. You look like someone else," said Hank. "Oh, I like it, how could anyone not like looking at you. You're smashing."

She blushed under the make-up.

"It's all in a day's work I guess."

"Look, I know that I want both you and Joan to take part in the modeling program. I'm sure of a few people, and you two are among them. I would like to have lunch with you to discuss how we are going to follow through."

"I've already had lunch."

"OK. then dinner. May I take you to dinner?"

"Joan too," she asked teasingly.

"No, I think that I can only take one of you beauties on at a time. Two of you together would overwhelm me."

Sally looked this gentle man. She really liked him. He was so warm and had been so kind to her. She liked him very much. She felt safe with him, safe from the terrible charges of electricity that seemed to surge through her whenever she met or even saw Brian. Safe from the fantasies that plagued her when she even thought about Brian.

After she had seen him leaning against her counter the other day, she had been so upset that she was barely able to work. She had gone through the day in a daze. The thought that the man whom she had fallen in love with might be Brian Lassiter, the owner of the store, was much too devastating to her. She had comforted herself constantly with the thought that he didn't know who she was and furthermore it was obvious, she hoped, that he had not recognized her. At the same time it bothered her that he hadn't.

But Joan could be wrong. After all she hadn't seen the man. All she had said was that the only Brian she knew was Lassiter, but that did not mean that the man who had been leaning against her counter had been he. Maybe he was someone else all together. Must be. She had said she believed that he was a much older man. Coming back to Hank, she felt the comfortable warmth again.

"Sure." she said, "I love to have dinner with you. But we're open until nine. I won't be able to leave until then."

"No problem, I'll meet you at the counter right after closing."

As soon as the losing bell had rung, and Sally had closed her register for the night, she made a bee-line for the Ladies' room. She couldn't wait to wash her face.

When she met Hank, he looked at her in surprise. "I can't keep up with you. Every time I see you, you look as though you were someone else. I liked the make-up. Why did you take it off?"

"Hank, I'm off duty now. This is really me, not the other plastic lady."

"Listen, honey, I know that you prefer the natural look, and fortunately for you, you can get away with it, but I'm afraid that you're going to have to wear it for the photographs."

"I don't mind, that's all part of work. That's OK. I'm beginning to like the fact that I look like two different people."

"Me, too. You've added another dimension to yourself. Now there are two people for me to love."

She glanced quickly at him.

"I hope that you're just kidding."

When he remained silent she added,

"You are, aren't you. I mean about love."

Abashed, he quietly said,

"Yeah, I'm just kidding. Right."

Abruptly he took her arm and swung into the avenue.

"Now where shall I take Mrs. Jekyll, or is it Mrs. Hyde to dinner."

Relieved at his abandonment of the earlier conversation, she pulled his arm closer to her, and smiled happily. The lovely warm evening echoed her mood as they went to a nearby little French restaurant.

"Jacques, good evening."

"M'sieur Rawls," he replied. "How are you this evening?"

"Do you have room for two more?"

"Naturellement, for you always."

He seated them at a table for two at the side of the room, Sally on the banquette, and Hank across from her.

The room was small, there were no more than about twenty tables and it was reputed to be one of the best French restaurants in town. Usually it was necessary to make reservations many days ahead, but Hank ate there so often that the practice was waived for him. One of the perks of his job was an expense account that no one thought to question. It was a good thing too, because it would have been very difficult for him to afford the prices of restaurant dining as often as he ate out. He liked good things, and fortunately his position allowed him to indulge himself.

There were black and white drawings of Paris around the room and on each pink tablecloth there was a perfect rose. Immediately after they were seated a waiter came over.

"Good evening, sir, madam, would you like a cocktail?"

"Just a glass of white wine for me please," said Sally.

"I'll have the same, and then may we have a menu. I think that we are both starved."

"What would you like, Sally?"

"You choose for me, I don't know much about French food."

Sally was hesitant because she had been given the Ladies Menu which had no prices. She didn't want to order anything too expensive but had no idea of what anything cost.

"We'll have trout farcie, côte de boeuf in Bordelaise with wild mushrooms and for dessert a crêpe soufflé à la Normande." He turned to Sally.

"Sound good?"

"Sounds terrific, I hope I can eat it all."

It really wasn't so unlikely that Brian should choose the same restaurant. After all it was very close to the store and it did serve some of the best food in New York. He had asked Mary to join him for dinner and they had come over to "La Frivolité." He, too, just signed the tab and the bill was sent over to the store for payment. So it was very logical that all four of them were in the same restaurant at the same time.

At first Brian did not see Hank and Sally as they were seated toward the rear. However, it was the captain who mentioned that Mr. Rawls and a very pretty lady were there as well.

Mary found them first. As they walked toward their table, she pulled Brian's arm,

"Look, there's Hank and that girl, Sally. She's pretty but sort of dull. You think that she would dress better. It wouldn't hurt to wear a little make-up. Some women think that they're so perfect that...."

"Shut up, Mary," Brian rudely interrupted.

Mary looked Brian in astonishment. He'd been unpleasant before, but he had never been rude to her in public. She blanched in anger.

"What on earth did I say to offend your highness?"

In answer he roughly turned her around and practically pushed her toward the door of the restaurant to the consternation of the staff. Mumbling some excuse, he slipped a bill into the captain's hand.

"M'sieur, have we done anything to offend?"

"No, nothing like that, I forgot something, that's all, I'll be back another day this week, Good night."

His held Mary's arm in a vise like grip as he forced her outside.

"What was that all about?" she asked as she clawed his arm away from hers. "You know Brian, that last weekend was no joy with you and tonight's behavior was horrendous. What on earth is wrong with you?"

He gave her a black look, turned away from her, and strode off down the street. She began to follow him and then furious in her turn, turned on her heel and ran to the corner looking for a cab.

After dinner, the weather was so balmy that Hank and Sally wandered home together, laughing and seemingly carefree. Sally enjoyed Hank so much. He asked nothing of her except her company and he sympathetically listened to all of her worries about the job. He was a good friend. However, she was aware of the fact that he was beginning to want to be more than that. As much as she wanted to really like him, there was a weight on her heart that would not allow her to be free. Every time that she looked into Hank's guileless eyes, she wished that they were not soft deep brown but rather those hard, penetrating sapphire eyes fringed by a curtain of black lashes, that she knew that she would never forget. She had been seared by them and she knew that she would always carry the scar caused by Brian. Brian, whoever he was, she knew that she would remember him forever.

"Sally I know that work means a lot to you. It should to everyone. A profession is something that you have to work and work at. I know all of that, but when it happens that there is nothing left other than that job of yours and an occasional date with someone, it is not good. You're getting too thin. I have a good mind to call your boss and tell him that you're working too hard. You're coming home so late from work. I know that this is an important project but...."

Sally interrupted her aunt with a hug.

"As usual, my darling, you worry too much. I work hard because I like to. I'm very pleased to have been asked to coordinate this new program with Hank. It's quite a feather in my cap and I enjoy it. They took me out of cosmetics at least to do this job."

"I know, and I'm thankful for that, at least you stopped looking like death warmed over with all of that make-up, but they should at least pay you for the hours you put in. I like Hank," continued Aunt

Helen. I'm happy when you bring him to dinner. He at least eats my cooking which is more than some others do."

"Nag, nag, all I get from you is nagging," Sally teased her aunt fondly. "You know that I never eat much when I'm caught up in a project. Look, it won't be too long. Hank says that as soon as we get the ground-work finished he'll show the whole thing to Mr. Lassiter and then we'll be on our way. I have to get all of the photographs finished of all of the staff and then they have to be collated and he and Mr. Lassiter are going to choose the most photogenic to do the ads and then the big contest. It's really such a good idea. Hank is proud of himself and he says Lassiter is too.

Mr. Lassiter has such faith in Hank that he just took off. Hank told me today that out of the blue he had decided to leave the whole project in Hank's hands and he only wanted to see the photographs when all of the decisions had been made. Hank doesn't even know where he is."

"Have you ever seen Mr. Lassiter?"

"No," Sally said as she carried over the plates to the small table where she and Aunt Helen would share their evening meal.

"I once thought that I did, but I guess I was wrong. Most people don't know who he is."

"Doesn't Hank know?"

"Of course, *he* does, but no one downstairs knows. He likes to sneak around and check up on people without their knowing it."

"That's disgraceful!" Aunt Helen was indignant. "He's like a spy. That's awful, I do not approve. I think that your Mr. Lassiter is not a gentlemen."

"Hank seems to think that it's all right. I mean it's not that he's spying, it's that he thinks that he can see how the store is operating without anyone putting "on a show for the boss" or something like that. Hank says he doesn't take advantage of people, but he wants to make sure that there is no sand in the cogs. Hank says that he's worked in every one of the departments, even cleaning lavatories over the years."

"I don't think that I'd like him. Come darling, dinner is ready." She carried over a bowl of rice. In another large serving bowl were piles of shellfish.

"That smells divine. What is it?"

"It's a Spanish dish. Clams, mussels, shrimps in what they call a salsa verde."

"Green sauce."

"Well, I'm glad you went to college, Lovey, right," Helen teased.
The smell wafted through the dining room.

"I just hope that this will tempt your appetite."

Sally looked sharply at her aunt and saw the worry on her face.
Although the odor was delicious, it didn't tempt her. No food had
since she had met Brian. It wasn't because the job was so demanding.
She vowed that she would do justice to the delicious meal into which
her aunt had put so much thought. She would do almost anything to
keep her aunt from worry.

It was true that Brian had taken off. No one knew where. Mary
wouldn't answer Hank. She disclaimed all knowledge when he had
pressed her.

"Do you really think that I am his keeper, Hank? How should I
know where or what he does. He called me and told me to tell you
that you should go ahead with the whole idea and he'll be back in a
week or two. I haven't the vaguest idea where he is."

After she had left Brian at the restaurant that night, Mary had
run to the corner to get a taxi. The night had been particularly warm
and balmy and she had hoped that it would have been conducive to
romance. His behavior had been so rude, so horrendous. She could not
remember any other time that he had acted that way. She knew that
he was moody. She knew that he was often morose, but in the past
she had always been able to lighten his moods when they became too
oppressive, but now it was as though she were compounding them. I
will not allow him to treat me like a fool. I am not a rug to be walked
on, in fact not just walked on but have the dirt ground into. I have
never given him cause to behave this way.

Mary was not a fool. She had worked her way through school,
modeling at times and she knew how hard New York life could be,
especially for an attractive woman. She knew what the temptations
were for both men and women on their way up. She knew that she
was good-looking, but she knew also that she was not as young as
she once was. It was through a lot of artifice and careful grooming
that she always looked attractive. She had given up a lot for Brian.
There had been men who wanted to marry her, but she had never
given up hope. And now an ugly thought came. In all of the years
that she had known him, there had never been any serious threat
to her as far as other women were concerned, but now, she had a

sneaking suspicion that somewhere there was someone who just might be the cause of his absolutely inexplicable behavior.

It was true that she did not really know the cause, and as hurt as she had been by his behavior, as angry and jealous as she was of the unknown threat to her, she was also worried.

IN THE INTERIM HANK AND Sally had organized everything. He had taken her off the sales floor. Her newest assignment was to spend hours and hours looking over travel brochures, looking for out-of-the-way romantic, exotic or exciting places. This part of the job was a lot of fun. Every day she would spend hours thinking of the places in the world that she would like to visit.

"Imagine, Aunt Helen, it's as though I have been offered the whole world. Anywhere in the world I want to go, I can. From Mount Everest to Death Valley, the Sahara, the Antartic, Europe, Mexico ... just anywhere. Hank is going to go as chief executive on the tour and he promised to take me as his assistant."

"Who else is going to go?"

"Well, whatever models are chosen. You know that's part of the contest that I told you about. The one with the greatest sales wins the trips. I think that they are planning about four girls and about the same number of men. And then there's Hank and me, and I guess that's all. They don't want too many because it's going to be prohibitive in cost."

Aunt Helen sniffed derogatorily.

"I should think with Lassiter's money, he could write Hank a blank check and never feel the pinch."

"That's probably true, but it has to make good business sense too. It's not only a question of being able to spend it, it's a question of projected return based on what you think the extra sales will bring in."

Helen looked at her niece fondly.

"My, you learn quickly. For a psychology major who couldn't balance her check book, you know a lot of economics and business."

"That's material that I've been learning with Hank. One of

the nice things about him is that he's nevertoo busy to stop and answer questions, no matter what they are, even if they seem silly, he considers them seriously."

"Does he behave that way with everyone?"

"I guess so. I never thought..."

"You're a smart girl, honey, I think that you must know that he cares a lot for you."

Sally blushed.

"I know that he does, Aunt Helen, but I'm just not interested. I'm fascinated by this business. The ramifications are tremendous. The opportunities are endless and I'm just not interested in becoming involved with anyone."

Her voice kept rising and she betrayed impatience as the words tumbled out. Aunt Helen looked at her in amazement. Wisely she held her tongue. It was not like Sally to lose her temper, certainly not about absolutely nothing. She suspected that everything was not all right with the girl. In her sensible way she knew that if she bided her time, eventually Sally would unburden herself. Meanwhile, she would always be there to provide comfort for her. I must keep a close watch until she does come to me though, but I won't push her.

The campaign was gaining momentum. All of the sales people were excited about the program and sales had never been better. As they had noted earlier there was a rise in morale. The whole store crackled with energy. They had only to count up the figures for a month to see who would win the contest. It was now in the second week and the figures were astounding. Hank was enough of a realist to know that the increase would be only temporary. It had been Sally's idea to make a contest of sorts an annual event so that they could get a boost every year.

She and Hank worked well together. After her initial stint at the cosmetics counter, he had decided that she would be more valuable to the store if she were to work with him exclusively. Both of them enjoyed the new situation. Hank because he cared so much for her and even more important, her quick mind and original ideas were of tremendous help. Time was very important now, and there were so many details to monitor that Sally became more than his amanuensis, she was becoming his full associate.

The only person that the situation did not seem to please was Mary.

"Why is it that every time that I ask Mary to type something for me or to take a letter, or in any way to help with my work she is so sullen? The first day that I met her she looked so sophisticated and sure of herself that she intimidated me. I envied her poise then, but now, I don't like her at all. She looks daggers at me when she sees me, and then she doesn't do what I ask of her. What have I done to offend her?"

After the store had closed for the day, Sally and Hank were going to meet the photographer to lay out some of the shots in the lingerie department. It was on the elevator that she asked this of Hank.

"I don't know, Sal. It must be that she's jealous of you."

"Me! Of what may I ask could she be jealous? She's beautiful, competent, knows the ropes, and I'm sure" she added teasingly "makes a lot more money than I do."

Hank grimaced in mock pain at her quip about her salary. It's true, he thought, no one should work sixty or more hours a week for the peanuts that she's being paid. But he said,

"Well, babe, you ought to be paying me for training you."

"Hah. This whole program is just a gimmick to get slave labor. I know your kind. The original exploiter!"

"You've got my number. I thought I'd be able to fool you forever."

"Kidding aside, Hank, I'll never thank you enough for this opportunity. I couldn't have learned all I have in the last few weeks if I had gone to school for years."

"Just think of me as your handy local College Dean. In answer to your question about Mary, I wouldn't worry about her too much. Something is bothering her and I don't think that it's just you."

"What do you mean, is it the extra work for the program?"

"No, I don't think so. I think that there's some connection between Lassiter's sudden disappearance and Mary's unpleasantness."

Hank realized after Sally had mentioned it that Mary had not missed a single opportunity to make a nasty crack or a dig about Sally. He hadn't thought much about it, but now that Sally had brought it up he planned to keep his eyes open. Hank was far from stupid and although Mary and Lassiter's relationship had not been common knowledge, he was aware that there was something between them.

He was as mystified as Sally though about the real cause of Mary's behavior.

When they arrived at the floor it was to find the photographer red-faced and almost speechless with rage.

"I cannot, will not work with this woman!"

Hank threw Sally exasperated look.

"What is wrong, Teddy?"

"Amateurs, that's what's wrong. I think that this whole idea is lousy. How can you run a campaign based on amateurs? I waste more time, I'm not interested in their ideas. They don't know anything except that they once posed for 'Daddy'. They think that that makes them experts. They get in my way. Give me a professional model any time. They keep their mouths shut, do what they're told. I don't want to work this way."

Hank took Teddy's arm and walked with him over to the end of the counter.

"Please Teddy, this program means a lot to me. Lassiter has given me a free hand with it, and if it fails, I fail. Help me. I'll work with you too. What really is the problem? I'm sure that the girls will work well if they know what we want. It might take a little time for them to relax and get into the swing of it."

"They talk too much. They don't want to be photographed in a slip and bra. 'It's too embarrassing,' they say. They want to hide behind the counter. Oh, I don't know, Hank, I don't think that it's going to work. He continued," Who is the girl who came up with you? She has such good bone structure. She would photograph beautifully if she can keep her mouth shut"

"Well, she can't be used because she's my assistant, she's never sold lingerie. It would ruin the whole thing, they have to be the real salespeople, don't you see, that's the gimmick for the campaign. Please try again, Teddy."

To Sally he said,

"Get that girl calmed down, explain again for the five hundredth time the whole strategy. See what you can do with her."

Sally put her arms around Gloria.

"I know it can be embarrassing, but the whole point is that we want to use the real people who sell lingerie. Sure, we could get one of the models who walk around half naked, but the whole difference is that we are using real people like you. Don't let the photographer bother you. He's just being temperamental. That's the way good artists are. It's not your fault. Try to relax."

Sally in her usual warm-hearted way, empathized with the girl's discomfort and did her best to cajole her into cooperating with Teddy. Between them they managed to calm both the photographer and Gloria, and after a while there were several shots finally accomplished but no one had the feeling that anything wonderful really had been achieved.

"I'll go back and print them, but I know they're not much good," said Teddy. "We'll have to think of something else."

"Well thanks, everybody," said Hank. "I know that it's hard to do this, particularly after a day's work. I'll look at the shots with you Teddy. We'll make a decision then. Do you think that we'll be able to see them tomorrow?"

Teddy nodded.

"OK Sally, let's go."

They rang for the elevator, neither interested in talking. Both were disappointed in the fact that the campaign seemed to have gotten off to a bad start.

"There's something wrong with the whole thing. I've been thinking that we need a more exciting locale," Sally said to Hank as he was sitting in the outer office the next morning.

"After all, the second half is going to be in exotic places, so maybe we should try for something like that here.

"You mean to take the photographs out of the store?"

"Yes, New York is really such an exciting city we could find interesting places all around town. Even the zoo could be used, the museums, ---."

And then Sally's irrepressible humor came forth again.

"What do you think about using a different model for the lingerie ads. There's a darling gorilla who might be persuaded to dress up in a bra and panties; if she's too uncomfortable we could always put a half slip on as well."

"No," Hank replied in the same vein, "it wouldn't work. The models have to be real salesgirls, and it has been against our policy to hire gorillas in the lingerie department."

"It is apparent to me, Mr. Rawls, that you have no sense of decorum."

"That's funny, you're not the first to say that."

"Really," said Sally in feigned surprise, "I can't imagine why anyone else would say that to you. You are Mr. Sobersides himself."

"You can be sarcastic if you like, Sally, my girl, but there are some people who think highly of me."

"Heavens, have I hurt your feelings, poor lamb." She grinned and grabbed his arm. "Come on, let's go out and scout up some really interesting locale. There's got to be a better way to do this thing."

"You are absolutely right, slave driver. You know, Sally, when I hired you for this job, I never thought that I would let you push me around."

"Push you around! Indeed. I am the one who works for slave wages, impossible hours, exhausted, I should report you to the ASPCA."

"If you were a gorilla, that would work, but there is no society to protect you. So I have you in my power. Ha, Ha, Ha."

"Come on Hank. We have work to do. The animal house awaits!"

Hank did realize the total effect Sally had on him. Aside from her beauty, her vitality was so great and her sense of fun so ready to explode, that he was smitten. He would at this time have done anything that she asked of him. As far as Sally was concerned, she knew that he liked her more than was good for either of them as she was not at all interested in him romantically. She considered him more as a delightful brother, and any time it looked as though there were an opportunity for him to tell her of his feelings, she did her best to make light of it or turn it into a joke.

So now she tried to get him back to the business at hand.

"Who told you that you had no sense of decorum?"

"Oh, that was Lassiter, the day I decided to hire you. He thought that it was unseemly to have so much levity emanating from my office."

"Did he say it in those words? Really like that? My goodness, he sounds stiff as a board!"

"No, not quite like that, but he didn't like it much."

"What is he like?"

"Well, I really like him a lot. I have a lot of respect for him. He's really very fair and works very hard himself." Suddenly he stopped. "I have it! I have the best, most romantic shooting location in the city, and it's right under our noses." He grabbed her hand and pulled her toward the elevator. When it came, he took out his keys and turned the lock on top of the panel.

"What are you doing? You'll turn on an alarm or something. Are there secrets in this building?"

"Just be quiet, old friend. Just look and don't say anything."

The elevator stopped at the penthouse and Sally found herself in the exquisite little lobby. Hank rang the bell to make sure that there was no one there. After a few minutes, during which time Sally devoured the delicate prints, he opened the door to Brian Lassiter's apartment.

He led Sally to the Japanese garden. She was speechless. He watched her eyes widen as she took in its delicate beauty.

"This place is ethereal," she whispered.

"What do you think? Could we use it?"

"I think it is the most beautiful place I have ever seen. What is it? To whom does it belong?"

"This is Brian Lassiter's penthouse. He designed it himself. He told me that it was all right to use it, but I had forgotten. Since he's not here, it would be a perfect time."

"I have never seen a more beautiful home anywhere. He must be a fascinating man. I would love to meet him."

"I'm sure you will some day. Listen, I have an idea. Teddy is taking pictures in the shoe department. If he's finished, I'd like to bring him up here and get his opinion. Wait here. Do you mind?"

"Mind? I could sit here forever. Go ahead."

Hank left. Sally entered the garden and strolled over to the bench which was set near the waterfall. Her light cotton frock moved gently in the soft breeze playing over the gravel. All of her senses were involved in the beauty of the scene. She was taken by the loveliness. The smell of jasmine permeated the air. She didn't know where it came from, it was just there. Sitting on the stone bench and watching the waterfall, she felt more at peace than she ever had in her whole life. Her face reflected the tranquil beauty of the garden and so when Brian Lassiter walked into his home and saw the embodiment of his dreams sitting in his garden, he felt as though he had been transported into another realm of consciousness. He stood enraptured, gazing at her beauty.

Unaware of his presence, she sat unmoving until a gasp rose from his lips. Startled by the sound, she turned toward him. As he crossed the garden in three huge strides, she rose from the bench, moving as though mesmerized, holding out her arms, convinced that she was

45

dreaming, that her desire had come true, that she had conjured up her lover.

Brian, too, thought that he was in a dream. There was no way that the woman with whom he fallen so deeply in love could be in his home. Sure that she was an apparition, he had no hesitation in embracing her, his anger and hurt nowhere in evidence.

She held him tightly and succumbed to a kiss deeper than she ever thought possible. He picked her up, murmuring words he did not know that he knew, terms of endearment, nonsense syllables. He crooned intermittently kissing her face and neck as he carried her through the doors that led to his bedroom.

Tears of joy were running down her cheeks and into the pillow as she prepared to be transported into bliss. It was ecstacy to be in his arms, and when he slipped the light cotton dress over her head, it was as though it were something that she had always known would happen, and had been waiting for forever.

"Sally, Sally, where have you got to?"

The magic of moment was torn asunder by the alien call of Hank Rawls. Brian flung himself backward with a curse. He raised his hand to strike the bewildered girl, who had been as shattered as he had been by the intrusion of reality in the person of Hank.

Brian recovering, quickly spat out,

"All of this time you thought I was Hank. You have sullied my home, you slut. You came here to make love to him, didn't you? Get dressed and get out!" He left the room, slamming the door loudly as he did so.

Sally lay there, uncomprehending the whole situation. She was trying to piece it all together when she heard Hank call again. I must be in a dream, I thought I was having the most beautiful dream in the world, but now I know that I am in the middle of a nightmare. This is reality. I don't know how I got into it, and I don't know how I am going to get out of it.

She dressed quickly, and ran out to the garden where she found Hank.

"Did you meet Brian?" he asked, "I saw his bags in the hall. He must have just come in."

Silently she stood there. Hank, unaware of the drama that he had interrupted, continued talking. "Teddy said that he would come up tomorrow. He's got too much to do now, and he doesn't want to stop. He is so temperamental, I hate to work with him, but he's so good. Incidentally, he asked again about you. He thinks that you would make a smashing model. He'd like to use you. Originally, we had thought that you would act as a salesgirl for something or other and I think that's a good idea. Just because you've been promoted to assistant is no reason that you can't do the modeling too." Misinterpreting her silence for unwillingness, he continued, "I'll let Teddy talk to you about it. He can be persuasive. Say, listen, I asked you if you had met Brian. He's got to be around somewhere. You said that you wanted to get to know him. I'll go find him. Shall I?"

"Please don't bother", she said in a voice so quiet that he had to bend over to hear, "I have met him."

"I MUST SAY, SALLY, THAT I don't really understand you. You seemed so happy in that job, you liked the people, you liked the excitement. You worked like a dog to be sure, but I thought that was because you liked it. What made you quit all of a sudden? It is not like you to do that. For absolutely no reason."

Aunt Helen was fixing the dinner that Sally probably would not even eat.

"Besides which, you are so thin now, you look like a scarecrow. You hardly eat anything at all."

"Models have to be thin. If you're not thin, you look fat. Cameras seem to put ten pounds on you."

"That's ridiculous!"

"Ridiculous, but true. I want to get these jobs, Aunt Helen."

"Well, it's beyond me. To be so thin that you don't look like a woman. You will look like a manikin, you won't look real."

Sally knew that Aunt Helen was right. She didn't like that emaciated look that was necessary to getting a model's job. She would much rather have continued as she was at Lassiter's, in the production department. But there was no way that she could have stayed on at the store after the incident with Brian Lassiter. Every time she thought what had happened that afternoon she turned rigid with anger. She had told Hank that she had to quit for family reasons. He had been on the phone every day to see if there were something that he could do to help with whatever the problem was, but she had refused to see him. Poor fellow, he had no idea of what had occurred. Not only was he saddled with the whole campaign, but he missed Sally terribly.

Sally did not want to have anything to do with that kind of work ever again, so when she remembered that Teddy, the photographer, had told her that she was photogenic and wanted to use her as a model, she had decided that it was a way to make a living. I will make a good deal more money than I was making at the store anyway. I'll be able to move out sooner and Aunt Helen can get to Arizona that much earlier.

She had tried to explain to her Aunt that there was no future in the store and she would never make enough money to move out. Aunt Helen didn't believe a word of it.

"Which of these pictures do you like?" Aunt Helen came over to the table to look at them. There was Sally in pose after pose; her hair swept up and one leg on a chair, Sally peeking behind her, in a cartwheel hat, in a negligee, in jeans, in a bikini She had spent the whole day with Teddy.

He kept saying, "You have the most fantastic cheekbones, no matter how I pose you, you look wonderful, you're a natural!" It was true that practically all of the shots showed her to be a beautiful girl. Aunt Helen, of course, thought that she was too thin in all of them.

"How can I tell which to choose? I always told you that you were beautiful, but you never believed me. You can see for yourself, there's not one in which you don't look terrific. Except, of course, you look though you need a good meal in all of them."

"Helen," Sally said warningly, "You are driving me crazy. That's the way I have to be. Please stop nagging. And anyway, it's just as well I'm not hungry most of the time."

She thought of the first day she had sat for Teddy. He had ordered lunch for both of them.

"Here you are, honey, a pastrami on rye and cole-slaw. Coffee black. I just doubled my regular order. I hope it's what you like." He sat down on one of the props. "Whew, I'm tired, but you! You're just great. I knew that you would be. Remember I told you so!"

"I can't eat, Teddy, I'm just not hungry."

"Listen, babe, you have to. You can't afford not to. Don't get crazy. There are a lot of crazies in this business. They stop eating to lose weight and then they can't eat at all. Anorexia, they call it. It's an occupational hazard."

"No, it's not that. I just don't feel like it."

He looked at her, quizzically. He knew that something had happened at the store and he thought that it had to do with Hank. As far as he was concerned it was a good thing because he liked Sally. As a matter of fact he liked her a lot, and now she was in his bailiwick, it suited him just fine. He'd seen a lot of beautiful women in his business. His business WAS beautiful women, but she was special. It takes more than just beauty to be a good model, he knew, and she had it. That was IT with a capital I and a capital T. Her sparkle, the hint of mischief in the deep eyes, even the pensive look, all promised more than just a pretty girl.

Even during the shooting when she looked sad, as soon as he said "ready" she gave off sparks as though she were plugged in. It was a special quality. There weren't many girls who had it.

"Listen, if you get too thin, you won't pay off my investment."

"Investment?"

"Yeah, I decided that if it's OK with you, I'll act as your manager. That way you save on pictures, portfolios, I get to take your pictures as your own photographer, no one could do it better than I can anyway and we'll split everything we make on your material."

He had gone on to explain that they could set up their own company and with his contacts, skill and her looks and personality, they could make a fortune. Sally thought that it sounded like a good idea, and so *Salted Ltd.* was born. For Teddy it was a sideline and for Sally it was work to do immediately.

"You know, Sal, every time I pose you in a different outfit or different hairstyle, you look different. I find it hard to recognize you from one shot to another."

"Well, what does that mean, that I'm a good model, or you're a good photographer?"

"I think that it is a little bit of both. You have to look very carefully to see that the same girl is in all of the pictures."

"Isn't it funny? I know that I look completely different when I wear make-up. I even fooled people who knew me well. They didn't recognize me at all. When I have that stuff on my face I become someone different."

She remembered the time that she had spoken to Brian at the cosmetic counter and he had not even recognized her.

As usual, the thought of Brian sent a shudder through her soul. The memory of that afternoon that had promised such bliss and turned into such a dreadful nightmare still haunted her. She tried to repress it but it kept flashing in her mind, causing her to blush even when she was alone. She remembered the touch of his lips, the caress of his hands. But his voice - she couldn't remember his voice. All of this emotion, this love for him that I felt is based on little more than chemistry - we have hardly exchanged words - we have never really talked. No wonder I can't remember his voice - I'm glad of that or I would hear him as well as see him and feel his touch in my dreams.

She shuddered with anger at herself and at him. How dare he have treated me that way - if I ever see him again - she clenched her fist - I want to hit him - to hurt him.

She was throwing all of her considerable energy into this new venture. She wanted a new career and no reminders of her stint at Lassiter's.

Teddy had decided that the time was right for their first gallery show. Sally was to help select the photos for the exhibit and work up a mailing list for the invitations. Teddy's was to take the pictures and contact his innumerable friends and acquaintances throughout the city. Sally, grateful for the fact that it left her no time to think except when she had collapsed into bed at the end of an exhausting day.

"I think that my hand is going to fall off if I address one more invitation," she moaned to Aunt Helen, and stretched her slim arms.

"There are about seventy more on the list. I'll finish them, why don't you go..."

"And have a nice hot bath," finished Sally, giggling.

Aunt Helen laughed a little defensively.

"Well, it couldn't hurt."

"I know, you old love. I think it's a great idea." She stretched again languidly, rose and gave her Aunt a big hug.

"I'm going to do just that."

Finally, the night of the opening arrived. She didn't have time for one of Aunt Helen's baths. She had been unable to find the right dress for the occasion, and it wasn't until late afternoon after scouring the city and trying on hundreds of dresses that she had found one that she liked. She took a quick shower and then put on make-up. She was used to wearing a lot of cosmetics now. It was as though the mask that she applied offered her anonymity. She became someone else underneath the creams and mascaras, shadows and lipsticks. She could let the face that she offered to the world be a different person than Sally.

Over the matching slip she let the dove-gray silk chiffon fall gently over her shoulders. It was so light it felt as though were wearing nothing at all. Long sleeved, it closed with four buttons at the wrist. The bodice, simple and high-necked, blended into the full skirt that draped gracefully over her slim hips. In her upswept auburn tresses she had pinned a pearl brooch but wore no other jewelry as the dress had a matching chiffon scarf which she draped over her shoulder.

Teddy, seeing a particularly attractive woman come into the gallery, walked over to greet her.

"Welcome, would you like some wine and cheese?"

Sally giggled, "Teddy, it's me."

"I can't believe it, Sally, of all people I should know your face better than anyone else. This is a you that I haven't seen yet, and baby it's the most beautiful one yet. You are breathtaking!"

"As far as I'm concerned, this face doesn't count as me. I feel like a paper doll that you can draw new faces on each time you want to get another person. What you see is someone else. Give the cosmetic companies the credit for the face, not Sarah Harte."

Teddy put his am around her.

"You're nuts. The most beautiful gal in town and with no ego to match. I can't believe it."

Sally walked over to the refreshment table. She was pleased with the way it looked. They had decided to stay with California wines and the selection ran from Sauvignon Vert, an excellent Sauterne, to a Chardonnay. They had Rosés and for those who wanted heavier wines, Zinfandels, Creme Sherry and for those who wanted nothing alcoholic, they provided soda and fancy imported water. The cheeses were varied as well. Ranging from Grueyres to Camembert, goat cheeses, and anything else a gourmet cheese store can provide.

She took a glass of soda and a small nibble of cheese, remembering as she did so that she had forgotten again to eat dinner. Teddy was worried that she was getting too thin and that it made her face look drawn. In spite of the fact that her face was going to be her fortune, Sally, as always, thought little of her looks. However, everyone else's eyes turned to her as they came into the room. Her coloring against the soft gray presented a lovely picture as she moved with unconscious grace through the gallery greeting people.

As the rooms became more and more crowded, she began to feel that the exhibit might just be a success and that their venture would work out well. As she stood next to the refreshment table a tall dark man in a fawn doeskin jacket brushed by, jostling her arm. Annoyed, she pushed his arm away as the liquid cascaded down the front of her lovely chiffon dress.

"Why don't you be more careful! Look what you've done!"

"I AM sorry but you were blocking the table and someone pushed me from behind. Let me help you." He whipped out an initialed handkerchief and started to blot her dress.

She realized that it was Brian, and thank goodness he didn't recognize her.

Coldly she said, "Never mind, you'll only make it worse. I can take care of myself, thank you."

Looking at her face for the first time, she saw his eyes widen. She was afraid it meant that he knew her, but it was only that he was struck by her beauty.

"I am truly sorry but, as I said, it was your fault too."

"My fault! I was standing still, and you were the one who moved and spilled the drink."

"Well, if you hadn't been hogging the table, you wouldn't have been pushed. Poor thing, I can understand why you have to stay near the food. Doesn't anyone feed you? You look like a starving waif."

Anger rose, pushing all other feelings aside.

"I think that you are the rudest man that I have ever met. Get out of my way, if you don't mind. Just who do you think you are?"

Intrigued by the spirit of this beauty whose eyes were flashing in indignation, Brian deliberately planted his feet apart and blocked her path. This was the first girl whom he had met that was able to push aside that nagging longing for that other; that woman whom he had vowed to forget. There was something familiar about her, but he couldn't quite place it.

Forgetting that she was to behave properly for her own as well as Teddy's sake, in her frustration, rage and hatred for Brian, she deliberately poured what was left of her soda down the front of his shirt, completely wetting it in the process. Then shouldering him aside, she stalked through the crowd without so much as an "excuse me."

Brian turned and followed her. When she came out of the lavatory where she had blotted much of the liquid from her dress, he was leaning against the door-jamb nonchalantly.

"It's my turn now. I have to repair the damage you did."

She passed him without a word, her chin in the air. So much for him she thought. He doesn't even recognize me. I can see how much our relationship had meant to him. He's ready to start with another woman. As a matter of fact, he probably has lots anyway and I meant nothing at all to him. He's a phony. Jealous of poor Hank. That's what that whole scene was about. Hank. What a joke. I can see now that the only thing that bothered me about that incident was the fact that I told him I cared for him. Never again. He used me. Well, I'm going to use him. I know who he is but he doesn't know who I am. We'll see who does what to whom now!

The exhibition had been a tremendous success. Teddy was rapidly becoming one of the most sought after photographers in the city and everyone wanted to know who his models were. Sally's name had never been introduced and now they had created mystery women. It had been part of their plan to capitalize on her protean quality and it was thought that Teddy had a stable full of models, all more beautiful than the next.

"Well, I'm certainly not type cast," she laughed as she realized the ramification of her anonymity.

"That's true, Sal, but do you realize that if you let your name be known, you could be one of the top models. I don't think that it's fair to you. You could be making a fortune."

"I guess so, but look what would happen if I did that. I would have to go out on my own and work for a whole lot of different photographers. I think we can do well enough this way. I prefer working with you anyway. It's much more fun. Some of those others are temperamental idiots."

"You thought I was too, until you began to work with me."

"Not really, I think you were in a tough situation at the store working with non-professionals."

"You got to be a pro pretty fast."

"It took a lot of work on your part too, Teddy, so don't sell yourself short. I don't think that anyone else could photograph me as well as you do anyway, so let's leave it at that."

They were sharing a soda after a morning's work. Sally was dressed in a loose smock covering a skimpy bathing suit.

"You won't be working at all next week, so get some rest while I am away."

"Are you going on vacation?"

"It looks like a vacation, but I think it's going to be an impossible week, and actually it's all your fault."

"Mine! How is that possible?"

"I got a call from Hank Rawls the other day. They are ready to go ahead with the final part of the campaign. Guess where they finally decided to go? They're going to do the whole thing in Mexico. It's got cities, beaches, ruins, pyramids, jungles. He's real excited."

"That was my idea," she said in a small voice. "I told him that was a place I always wanted to go. I've always loved the Mayan culture, whatever I've read about it. Absurdly, she was jealous. "I wish I could go."

"Look, kid, I don't know why you quit the store, but why couldn't you go? Did you have fight with Hank? Anything like that?"

"I quit. I wouldn't go back."

"But you didn't quit me. So you come too, if you want. You could be my special assistant. As a matter of fact, there's no reason that we couldn't get some good shots of you down there too. We could use them for the next show, or whatever."

Teddy was very fond of Sally. She was good company and a hard worker. There was no reason that she couldn't go. She could use the sun and it would be good for her.

"Mexico City, too? I must admit I'm sorely tempted."

No longer afraid of her feelings for Brian, her anger had triumphed over all of her other emotions. There's no reason not to go, she thought to herself. It would be fun. Teddy was a good friend and she would not have too much trouble, she felt, keeping Hank at bay. As a matter of fact, he's probably forgotten all about her too. Men! She thought inconsistent, unworthy and disloyal.

Mexico City was very bit as beautiful as Sally had imagined. Their hotel was right on the Reforma, a tremendous avenue separated by islands of trees and plantings which ended at Chapultepec Park. Across the paseo was the Zona Rosa, where there were lovely shops with vast collections of clothing and jewelry. A people's market had hundreds of little stalls where you could buy anything from a side of beef to beautiful silver tea services. Wandering around the city could have taken all of Sally's time, it was so fascinating, but there was work to do. She and Teddy had come down before Hank was to arrive with the lucky winners of the contest. They had to find some interesting locations for the photographs. The city itself was so photogenic, it would be hard to find bad locations. That morning they had gone to the Anthropological Museum in Chapultepec Park.

"It would be absolutely incredible to pose the girls in this court yard with the fountains playing in front of that huge stone statue."

"What is that? It's enormous. It would make a terrific shot."

"It's Coatlicue, Mother God of the Mexicans."

"Stand in front of it." Teddy framed Sally with his hands. She was wearing a Mexican dress of white cotton, embroidered with red and yellow flowers along the shoulders and neck. Her red hair burnished by the sun, tumbled free over her shoulders.

"Sally, I don't know which girls Hank is bringing down, but whoever they are they won't be able to compete with you."

"Any pictures we take of me will be for our own purposes. Don't forget, the girls who are going to pose have to be the winners of the contest."

"I don't forget that at all. I just want you to pose there again for me."

He knelt and ducked down, stood, crouched and swung from one side to the other. As often as Sally had seen the contortions necessary to get a picture, sometimes Teddy's actions and facial expressions couldn't help but amuse her. She laughed aloud.

"Great," he shouted, "that's great."

His antics were more than hilarious as he climbed on to the ledge of a pillar. A fierce looking guard with bristling black mustachios rapidly approached him and in no uncertain terms made sure that he understood he was not allowed to touch or climb on anything.

When they got to the hotel, they found a phone message. Hank was not going to be coming to Mexico City at all. He had been held up at the store with some serious problems. Instead, Mary was going to be in charge of the salespeople- models, the winners of the contest. Would Teddy take charge of everyone until Mary and Brian got there? Hank would try to meet them at the later locations if it were at all possible.

Sally blanched. Brian and Mary coming here. This was going to turn into a nightmare. Aloud she said to Teddy,

"I'm very tired all of a sudden. Would there be time for a rest before dinner?"

"Of course, go up to your room and stretch out. You have hours and hours since no one eats dinner here before nine o'clock. Don't forget the altitude is hard to get used to so you have to expect that you will tire much more easily. Sleep well and dress pretty."

"What would be appropriate, do you think?"

"Well, the nights are cool, so a suit would be perfect."

Sally took the elevator to the tenth floor which gave her a marvelous view of the Paseo de la Reforma. She could see the parklike boulevard stretching for miles. What a beautiful city, she thought. I hope it's not going to be spoiled by Brian's presence. I hope that he doesn't recognize me. And Mary too. That woman gives off unpleasant vibrations but I never understood why. She dozed off, her thoughts, chasing each other, of Brian, Mary, spilled drinks, art galleries, statues and cameras.

She woke to the shrilling of the phone, and for a moment did not know where she was. She groped for the instrument.

"Sally, it's Teddy. I seem to have inherited Hank's role as the head of this expedition. Time to wake up. I'll meet you in an hour in the lobby."

She stumbled to the bathroom, yawning, and filled a bath with hot water and poured in some French bath oil. The clouds of aroma filled the room. Lowering herself into the tub, she thought about how lucky she was. This was going to be an adventure in one of the most beautiful cities of the world. She was going to see places she had only read about, eat fascinating foods, see pyramids - imagine - pyramids. She luxuriated in the warm water, and then remembered! Brian and Mary were going to be here too.

She knew that he hadn't recognized her last time they met at the gallery, but would she be able to keep him from knowing who she was when they were going to be spending so much time together? It means that I have to wear makeup all of the time. I hate that, but I think it's the only way I can keep him from knowing me. Of course, it's entirely possible that he forgot that other Sally all together. That bastard! He probably has. Her thoughts alternated between wishing that he had forgotten the incident in the Japanese garden and wanting him to remember it forever.

She dressed carefully in a soft suede plum-colored suit, with a striped silk blouse picking up the colors of the leather. After braiding her long red hair she pinned it into a coronet and put on antique gold dangling earrings which Helen had given her. After toying with the idea of false eyelashes she decided against them. Too much is too much! It is not worth that torture even if I am unmasked. It's enough too have to endure all of this face paint.

When she stepped into the lobby, there was not a man who who did not notice her. As unconcerned as usual about her effect on people, she hurried over to Teddy and kissed him on the cheek. He held her away from him, gazing at her face.

"I've never seen your hair like that. You look like a princess."

She laughed, and brushed his jaw lightly with her palm.

"Some princess, I'm as hungry as a peon. I'm not used eating so late."

"I've made reservations at a marvelous place. It's an old convent. Wait till you see it. I hear it's one of the most beautiful restaurants in Mexico, and the food is as good."

She looked around nervously and said,

"Where are the others? Aren't they coming too? After all they are in charge of the whole thing now, we're just the unimportant help."

Teddy, misinterpreting her concern, thought that she was worried about his having brought an extra person.

"Don't worry, I told Lassiter that I brought my assistant. He said that it was just fine. He doesn't have to worry about bucks, you know."

"I know, but does he know who your assistant is? Did you say it was me?"

"No, he doesn't know and I'm sure he doesn't care. You don't know him anyway, so what difference does it make?"

"Right, Teddy," she echoed, "What difference does it make? But listen, Teddy, call me Sarah from now on."

"I'll call you anything you like, but why 'Sarah'?"

"I feel like a Sarah here. Sally isn't dignified enough."

"OK, Sal - ahem, I mean Sarah. Anything you say. Anyway, we're to go ahead, and they'll meet us there."

When they arrived at the old convent, Sally was taken by the beauty of the old building. It wasn't until they entered and she caught a glimpse of the inner rooms that she would have known that it was a restaurant. The courtyard was planted with hundreds of flowers, all giving off a magnificent scent.

"Sally, I mean Sarah, I want to tell you um, I'm becoming more than a little fond of you, do you think..."

"Oh look," she interrupted quickly. To herself she thought, oh please, let Teddy keep our relationship on a business basis. I just need a good friend. Let him be no more than that. Aloud she said as she moved a little to the left,

"There's our company now."

Mary, stunning and impeccable in a black silk suit and a white silk blouse, pearl earrings and black sandals, led the group. Sally didn't recognize any of the salespeople who had won the contest, but following the group and obviously in command was Brian.

Her heart dropped at the sight of his tall figure, beautifully dressed in a tight-fitting European styled suit, the lines of which showed off his lean body.

The maitre'd seated them at a large round table. Brian smiled in greeting to Sally and offered his hand to Teddy, helped Mary into her seat, and placed himself between Mary and Sally..

"Teddy, since you are the only one here who knows everyone, why don't you make introductions."

Willingly Teddy obliged. He introduced everyone including his assistant "Sarah Harte."

Brian looked quizzically at Sally.

"Haven't we met? You do look so familiar."

Her heart lurched, but Teddy said,

"It's more than likely that you met at the gallery the night of our exhibit."

Brian smiled, as his eyes twinkled in recognition.

"Yes, indeed, I remember well. The soda girl! Perhaps this interlude will be even more sparkling than I had anticipated."

Sally blushed as Mary sharply glanced at Brian's face, then lightly placed her arm on his. Sally, furious with herself that Mary's gesture should annoy her, set her lips and pointedly ignored him.

As hungry as Sally had been she found that the presence of Brian and Mary was unsettling. Initially she found it difficult to eat the food but no matter how upset she was, she could not resist the dish that consisted of a crepe filled with chopped meat delicately spiced, and topped with nuts, sour cream and caviar. It was ambrosia! Brian, knowledgeably, ordered Mexican wines.

"I always try to order wines from the country in which I am. You'd be surprised at the excellent wines I have found. Mexico has some delightful vintages."

He directed his words to Sally.

"I'd like you to try this '73. I have to wean you away from soda water. Perhaps you would be less dangerous."

"I don't care much for alcohol."

"But this you must try."

"Just because you are financing this expedition doesn't give you the right to tell me what to drink," she said with more than a touch of asperity.

"If you want to remain a small town girl all of your life, go ahead, but you never know what you're missing until you've tried it."

"Small town indeed. I was born and raised in New York."

"Somehow, you seem to have missed some of its finer qualities," he said blandly. Turning to Mary he said,

"May I give you some of this delicious wine. It's probably too sophisticated for our neighbor anyway." He carefully poured out the clear ruby liquid.

Deliberately, Mary raised the glass to her lips and sipped it delicately.

"Ummmm, it's very complex, and it certainly has a good nose. Excellent. Really excellent."

She smiled appreciatively at Brian.

"That was a fine choice."

She again laid her small hand on his arm possessively.

Sally fumed. He had won that round. He had succeeded in making her feel gauche and uninteresting. She was annoyed at herself as well for the anger with which she watched Mary and him talking earnestly together. She fervidly threw herself into conversation with Teddy, deliberately angling her body so that her back was toward Brian.

However, Brian was not going to let her go.

"Excuse me, Sarah, would you lean back a little. I haven't had a chance to talk with Teddy."

Annoyed at the familiarity with which he tapped her arm, she leaned far back against the banquette. He moved closer to her letting his thigh touch hers. He couldn't be unaware of the pressure of his leg against mine, she raged inwardly. Impatiently she moved over so as not to be in contact with him.

He turned toward her,

"Am I crowding you? I am so sorry."

However, be made no attempt to move away. He then launched

into a long discussion with Teddy about the locations that he had considered. Angrily she stared ahead. How dare he literally push me around. It's as though he thinks that he owns me. She was not unaware of the pleasure she felt as his thigh had touched hers and remembered again that ecstatic afternoon. Furiously she willed herself to stop thinking that way.

"Would you mind, Mr. Lassiter. It's quite uncomfortable. I'm being squeezed to death between you. Why don't you move closer to Mary?" She smiled coldly into devilishly blue eyes.

"Oh yes, Mary. Let me introduce you to Mary."

"Mary," he tapped her on the arm to attract her attention, "this young lady wants to meet you."

Unthinkingly, she slammed her knee into his leg.

"I'll get you for that," he whispered into her ear. "That's a very pretty ear. I'd love to nibble on the lobe." Ignoring her rage, and the pointed elbow she jabbed him with he said,

"Mary, this is Sarah."

"Yes," said Mary coldly, "I heard her name, Brian."

"Now be nice, Mary," he said in the tone one would use to a bad dog. "She's a nice girl. So you be nice. No teeth, no growling. Secretaries are not supposed to growl."

Mary turned her back on him as well in exasperation. She never knew how to handle Brian when he was in one of his unpredictable moods.

She had been surprised that he had invited her to come along on this jaunt with him. It was the first time in weeks that he had spent any time with her at all. Her official role, of course, was secretary but she hoped that she would be able to regain some of the ground that seemed to have been lost with Brian. He had seemed so remote ever since he had disappeared last month. And now, she felt de trop. She could see he was interested in that young girl. How could she compete with anyone who looked like that! The girl, fortunately, seemed not to be interested in Brian at all. It was the first time that she had ever seen anyone being deliberately cold to him. Not that he didn't deserve it. His rudeness was a blatant display of interest in her. She'd seen it before with other women. They had come and gone. It was a good thing that Sarah did not see it that way; she just thought that he was uncouth. Nevertheless, I have to keep on my toes, she thought. I hope that the trip doesn't turn into a fiasco. If Brian doesn't get what he wants, he'll be horrible to be with. If he does get what he wants, I have lost again. I wish that I could fulfill all of his needs. Life would be so simple. She turned back again to Brian hoping to attract his attention. However, he was talking to Teddy while pointedly ignoring Sally; yet unseen by the others, he had rested his hand on her thigh.

"Excuse me." Sally attempted to rise. "I would like to go to the ladies' room."

Brian held her arm.

"Can't you see that other people have to get up to let you out. Can't you wait," he scolded.

Angrily Sally said,

"No, I can't", and attempted to push past Brian, furious that he seemed to try to control her in every way possible. Mary had to get up and move out and Brian too had to move to the end of the banquette. Wishing that she had the nerve to slap his hand as it had lain on her leg, she settled for deliberately stepping on his foot as she edged past him.

"I'll join you," said Mary.

"Good idea, keep an eye on her, she's obviously unstable," Brian laughed.

"I can't get over the feeling that I've seen you before," Mary said as she touched up her already perfect lips. "Have I?"

Sally's heart slipped. She had banked on Mary's not connecting her with Lassiter's.

"Perhaps you met me at the gallery. Were you at the exhibition with Brian?"

"Not likely. Brian and I don't socialize together. I am just his secretary," she said tightly.

Sally heard the bitterness and knew that that might be the case, but it certainly wasn't the status that this beautiful but cold woman would like to have. The feeling of antipathy was so thick it was almost tangible. She realized that Mary was an enemy whom she disliked as much as Mary seemed to hate her. It was when she was faced with the fact that Mary was a potential rival for Brian's affections that she was willing to admit openly to herself that she would always be involved with this capricious man, whose actions were incomprehensible to her. She remembered the touch of his hand on her thigh and how conflicted her feelings were. She wanted to press it harder against her skin and yet that he dared to touch her had made her long to slap it away.

This is going to be more than I had bargained for. I don't think I can handle this trip. Maybe I'll just go home. I can find an excuse.

They rejoined the others in time for coffee and dessert.

"May I suggest something to you, or would you consider that too, to be demeaning," Brian said laughingly.

"Thanks, I just want coffee."

"Stubborn. What a foolish girl. Doesn't want to learn the finer things," he mumbled infuriatingly to himself but loud enough for Sally to hear.

"I never eat dessert, thank you." To herself she sullenly added, I wouldn't take your suggestions anyway. Go tell it to Mary. Surprised at the childishness of her reactions she smiled at her own behavior. Suddenly the whole situation struck her as being ridiculous and she began to laugh.

Her laughter was so captivating that everyone at the table was infected. No one, of course, knew what was the cause of her mirth and every time anyone tried to ask her, she burst into a new siege of hysterics. When she finally calmed down Brian handed her a glass of wine, which she swallowed unprotestingly. Surprised by the warmth that flowed through her, she turned to look at him. Suddenly subdued, she softly said,

"Thank you. You are right. The wine is lovely"

Smiling in victory, Brian laid his arm across the back of her seat, seeming carelessly to allow his hand to touch her shoulder. Annoyed at his intimate gesture, yet wishing at the same time that he would hold her closer, she did and said nothing.

"Finish it like a good girl now," he spoke softly. "I think there are many lessons for you to learn. I am a really good teacher. You could be a good pupil, if you let yourself."

The superiority in his tone was enough to annoy her again. She moved closer to Teddy and said aloud,

"I think that it's time to go, don't you Teddy?"

"It isn't up to me, Sarah, I just work here. And, incidentally, so do you."

"Not true! No one owns me or my time! As a matter of fact, I might just quit."

"Hush now, don't spoil a good thing, Sal," Teddy whispered. "Our next shots tomorrow are going to be at the pyramids near here. And after that we're going down to the Yucatan. And don't forget, we're not paying anything for what could be a fantastic experience. The

Mayas, Mérida, soft beaches, scuba, sailing - you name it, we can do it and all in the name of photography."

"Fantastic experience," she shot back. "All in the control of a monster."

"What are you two whispering about," interrupted Brian. "Why don't we have our brandy in the courtyard? It's very romantic."

Sally shrugged indifferently.

"Whatever you say, obviously you are the big boss around here."

Teddy pinched her gently and whispered,

"Don't push him too far. We need him more than he needs us."

Sally turned to glare at him.

"I don't need anybody!" She threw her head back and walked out of the room, leading the rest of the party. But as they entered the scented courtyard, she was reminded of the smell of jasmine in that Japanese garden and she longed to have Brian hold her in his arms once more. But she would never let it happen again convinced as she was that he cared nothing for her. Indeed, he can care for no woman because he's so involved with himself. A conceited devil! In love with himself, he uses everyone to his own advantage. I dislike myself for being a fool almost as much as I dislike him. How can I care for such a heartless, eccentric and overbearing man!

As much as she did not want to have the brandy that Brian offered in that seductive courtyard, she found that she had actually enjoyed the Felipe Segundo that was served. The velvety liquid slid down her throat effortlessly and she smiled in appreciation.

"Hah! a convert! I thought that you didn't care for alcohol, and here you are drinking. You see, you instinctively know what is good. That is one of my favorite brandies. I prefer it to the more highly touted French. You just have to stay with me Sarah, my dear, and I'll teach you all of the good things in life, you poor provincial pussycat."

Mellowed by the alcohol her feistiness dissolved. She beamed on the assemblage, her double dimples emphasizing the beauty of her smile. Surprised and touched by this change of character, Brian suddenly withdrew from her vulnerable amiability. Under his breath he murmured,

"The brandy seems to have de-clawed you my beautiful lioness.

No more toying with you tonight." He turned to Mary and caressed her arm.

"Did you enjoy dinner?"

"This place is beautiful and the food was wonderful," replied Mary, "who wouldn't? Only unsophisticated people with unsophisticated taste, I guess."

"Time for the evening to end, everyone. Work tomorrow!" His abrupt change in mood startled all of the group, but obediently they got to their feet as he shepherded them out to the cars.

Sally fell asleep quickly. But unaccustomed to alcohol as she was, she slept restlessly. She dreamt all night of Brian. The many different Brians that she knew. The Brian in the park that first time that they held each other and told each other that they cared, the Brian of the Japanese garden, the beauty of the afternoon and the horror with which it had ended, the Brian at the gallery and her pouring soda on him and now this new, this completely unpredictable Brian. Even in her sleep she was troubled by the fact that she wasn't sure if he knew that Sarah was Sally.

She woke the next morning tired. It had been a bad night. Looking in the mirror as she started her toilette, she saw a bleary-eyed girl with mauve circles under her eyes and new lines around her mouth. I hope that Teddy isn't planning to shoot me today. This would be one more Sally that no one could recognize, she laughed to herself, and I hope indeed that no one ever would, I look terrible! I don't think that alcohol is for me. I really knew better, but Brian shamed me into it. As she slipped into the hot tub, Aunt Helen's prescription for whatever ails you, "It couldn't hurt," she heard her say. By the time she had finished bathing, her breakfast had arrived and been set up at the window table overlooking the Reforma.

Her spirits rose in direct proportion to the hot coffee and orange juice that she consumed. I could drink a gallon of that fresh Mexican juice. By the time she had had her third cup of coffee, she was ready and excited to face the day and whatever it held in store. I will not let that man intimidate me. As a matter of fact it tickled her to think that Brian was paying for a vacation that she could have never afforded any other way. I'm going to have a good time whatever happens, she vowed, but I wish that he would just go away. As quickly as that thought appeared, it was chased by her thinking that she would hate it if he really did leave.

After making up carefully, particularly under the eyes, she combed her hair in the style of a Spanish señorita, pulled back in a low bun and added a pair of wide silver hoops that she bought in the Zona Rosa. A black cotton blouse embroidered with fuchsia red flowers and a black cotton skirt completed the striking outfit. It's funny, she thought, how my tastes in clothes have changed. I used to dress so conservatively. Working around the fashion industry really has opened my eyes. It was true. Her style was much more adventuresome than it had been when she had first gone to Lassiter's to apply for the job. She wasn't afraid to try new hairstyles or new types of jewelry. She had gained in poise, and was feeling more comfortable. Although she still didn't take much time in dressing, she did try new things. She still was not particularly impressed with her looks. If she were to think of them at all, it would be simply to say that she was an average looking woman. Not beautiful and not ugly. Just passable.

It was not the opinion of the men in the lobby as she came out of the elevator. Everyone turned to look at the sprightly young woman who strode into the front of the hotel with such seeming assurance. She had no hesitation in smiling at those who smiled at her. She was full of the beauty of the day and felt the magic of Mexico. She was ready for whatever adventure today was going to bring. Looking around for Teddy but unable to see him in the lobby, she went outside only to be faced by the unblinking eye of his camera.

She broke into a wide smile as she saw him crouched into one of his uncomfortable positions. He kept snapping her as she walked toward him.

"Stop, you idiot, you're going to back into the street," she called out in alarm and ran toward him to halt his crablike progress.

"You're impossible," she scolded. "You'll kill yourself one day trying to get that 'one last shot.'"

He put his arms around her which was difficult since three cameras made for a very uncomfortable embrace and brushed her hair with his lips.

"For you it would be worth dying. That 'one last shot' would guarantee me entrance to heaven without question."

"You're crazy," she laughed, moving his arms away.

"I waited outside for you because I wanted to see if I could catch you completely unawares. I think that I got some good stuff that time. Together we're a terrific team."

Sally glanced at him quickly. Teddy was so comfortable. So predictable, so warm and so nice. It would be so easy to have a relationship with him. So easy and yet absolutely impossible. Not as long as Brian existed.

To Teddy she said,

"It's you who has the genius. You can photograph anything. That's the art. I could just as well be a peach or a pear on a table. Models are a dime a dozen."

He hugged her to him.

"Not like you, honey. Not like you."

"Well, excuse me. Are we intruding on this tender little scene? What do you think of public displays of emotions, my dear?" Brian turned to Mary, "You wouldn't indulge in anything like that, would you? You're too much of a lady." And to Teddy and Sally he said,

"Have you two quite finished or are you planning on embarrassing me some more?"

Sally flushed with anger at his unprovoked attack, while Teddy just played with his cameras.

"I wouldn't deign to explain myself to you." She turned on her heel away from Brian and took Teddy by the arm. How was it possible that that horrible man could manage to ruin her every happy feeling.

Brian tapped his foot impatiently.

"Mary, did you order the limo? I thought that you said it would be on time. Can't you do anything right?"

Patiently, Mary pointed at the waiting limousine.

"Get in the back, all of you." he ordered. "I will sit in front with the driver."

Sullenly Sally turned her face to the window and listened intently while the driver gave them a guided tour of the city. It had been decided last night that they were going to the Pyramides de San Juan Teotihuacan. Of course, Brian had been here before as he had been to most places in the world, and it was his idea that they would be able to get some interesting photos using the Pyramids as a background for the models. Teddy, of course hoped he could catch Sally in a few shots unbeknownst to Lassiter.

They were old structures built between 400 and 800 AD. No one is really sure of their absolute purpose, but most feel that they were religious centers for the Toltec Indians. Why they were abandoned is a mystery. The Pyramid of the Sun is over two hundred feet high and the base is more than 700 square feet. It is actually a series of pyramids, built on top of one another. A smaller pyramid, the Pyramid of the Moon, is on the thoroughfare called the Avenue of the Dead. It is possible to climb the structures and they hoped that they could take photos at the top. The broad street ends at the Temple of Quetzalcaotl, The Plumed Serpent, where there are magnificently preserved carvings of the Plumed Serpent and Tlaloc, the Rain God. Teddy hoped that these, too, would be excellent locales for his own photographs.

There was a pall on the spirits of the passengers in the car. Sally wished that they could have gone there without the overbearing presence of Brian. He didn't say a word to anyone, even when they went through the zoo at Chapultepec Park to see the Pandas. Sally couldn't resist their charm and Teddy insisted on a few shots with them as well.

"Don't forget, Teddy, your primary purpose is to take pictures of Peggy and Marian, Bob and Roy. If Sarah is your assistant, you'll have to use her properly for my purpose. Not to take photos of her. She is not my model."

Teddy flushed and said nothing at this tongue lashing, but managed to sneak in pictures of Sally whenever he was able to without Brian being aware.

"If I didn't know that he had a heart of ice, I would think that he's jealous of my being with you."

"Nonsense," she said. "He's so in love with himself that he couldn't care about anybody. Everything has to be his way. I bet if he wanted a woman and she finally wanted him in return, he would drop her like a hot potato. He just likes to try out his power on people. He has no heart."

This conversation took place as Teddy and Sally were walking ahead along the Avenue of the Dead. They had finished for the morning and were going to have lunch in the restaurant overlooking the Pyramids.

"He doesn't seem to be getting anywhere with you," said Teddy. "You don't give him the time of the day."

"What's more," she retorted, "I never will."

"But don't forget, he's paying our way."

"Teddy, you sell yourself short. You're here because you're doing a job, and it will be the best that he can buy. He's not about to let you go no matter what I do. Besides, you need me, and he's not going to let me go because you do need me."

"Sally, I do need you in more ways than one."

"Teddy, stop. Please stop. We're good friends, and I would like to keep it that way. Please."

She turned to face him and put her hands on his shoulders, looking deeply into his eyes."

"Whatever you say, babe. Just always know that the more time I spend with you, the more I want to spend."

"Thanks. I'll never forget that, Teddy. And know that it means a great deal to me that you feel that way, but I don't want to be involved with anyone. Please, let's stay friends."

She kissed his cheek and turned to enter the restaurant.

"Can't you keep your hands off each other? Your behavior is juvenile, if not downright in poor taste."

Sally turned in her tracks. "(A), our behavior is our business; (B), you pay for our time and our work, not our feelings; (C), you haven't the vaguest idea of what you're talking about," she pushed him aside; "and (E), I am not interested in joining you for lunch. I'd prefer to spend the time climbing the pyramid."

She turned on her heel and flew back down the Avenue.

Teddy called out after her, "Be careful Sal. It's easy going up, but it's very hard to come down. The steps are so shallow you have to place your feet sideways."

Sally ran down the Avenue of the Dead all the way to the Pyramid of the Sun. She was furious with Brian and angry too with Teddy for having put her into the position of being embarrassed. That Brian should make her feel this way is the thing that was the most infuriating. Why should she care what he thought about her? After reaching the base of the massive structure, she started up without looking back until she reached the top. It was only then that she looked down, and realized how steep the descent would be and wondered how she was going to manage. It was precipitous. There were no railings and she saw how foolish she had been. Why should I punish myself because I am angry at him! I think I'll sit up here and look at the incredible remains of this ancient city. I'm delighted that my anger drove me up to the top. What a place this must have been! It's hard to imagine a complex city built so long ago. After she had calmed herself thinking about the ancient Toltecs, and deciding that it would be too difficult to photograph the models she slowly and very carefully picked her way down the steep shallow steps. When she reached the bottom, she found that Teddy was waiting for her.

"If you hurry, oh important one, we're about to go to Xochimilco."

Having worked off her anger she was once again her charming self. She greeted the others in the limousine as though nothing had happened. Looking forward to the fabled floating gardens she sat forward in anticipation, looking at everything on the way. She wasn't even annoyed at Brian's seemingly endless store of knowledge, which he had no hesitation in displaying.

"Do you know that the Floating Islands are called that because they were originally built by the Aztecs? As the Valley of Mexico became crowded by their population expansion, they built dirt-covered rafts on which to plant their crops. The rafts took root in the shallow waters and became the islands which we will now see. - Here we are now."

Boat after boat was tied up at the side of the canal. They had to walk over many of the flower-bedecked rafts before they came to one that was free. Expertly, the gondolier poled them out into the narrow canals. Mariachis played and sang typical songs as they floated by. The whole atmosphere was fun-filled and light.

Brian was pleasant to everyone. He made no comments to Sally, nasty or otherwise. It was not exactly as though he were ignoring her, but rather that she was deserving of no special notice.

"Oh look," she called. "There's a boat that sells food."

One of the vessels had been poled alongside theirs. On a charcoal stove tacos filled with meat and vegetables were cooked right in front of them. Sally, who had not eaten, was hungry by this time.

"Would you like something," asked their gondolier.

"Oh yes, I'd love a taco. They smell so marvelous."

"Chicken or beef, Señorita?"

"Chicken, and I'd like a soda too."

The gondolier pulled out a plank and set it up between the two rows of seats creating a table making it comfortable to relax and enjoy the food and the beauty of Xochomilco. The odors were so tempting that the others decided to join Sally.

Indian women floated past, offering bunches of roses grown on the island. Brian signaled to the flower boat which poled over and he bought bunches of roses all the women in his party. A carnival air prevailed. All memories of early unpleasantness seemed to have been forgotten.

In the limousine going back to Mexico City, everyone was quiet. It was a comfortable quiet born of happy tiredness and remembered pleasure. Sally sat next to Teddy and fell asleep against his shoulder. Brian glanced into the rear-view mirror occasionally, although he never turned around to observe them directly and made no comment at all. Once in awhile, however, he would clench his fists and his brow would furrow.

THE YUCATAN! SHE HAD BEEN wanting to go to the Yucatan ever since she had read about it years ago. She fell asleep twisting the strange Mayan names over her tongue, Uxmal, Chichen Itza, Quintana Roo, Cozumel - she couldn't wait until tomorrow.

Brian had chartered a small plane for the next few days. Their first stop was Merida, the "Paris of the West" so called by the wealthy citizens of the small city.

The rich sent their children to Paris for education and their own diversion as it was so much easier to travel by ship to Europe than to try to cross the impenetrable jungle to the rest of Mexico. During the hey-day of sisal production there were many wealthy plantation owners. Now that synthetics have taken over the rope industry, Mérida's fortunes had declined. Some reminders of this wealthy period are the magnificent mansions that line Avenida Montejo. The sophisticated city is in great contrast to the thick jungle which surrounds it.

They had hired three "Calesas," horse-drawn carriages in which to tour the small city.

"It could almost be 19th century Paris," observed Brian. He had arranged that he, Mary and Sally shared a vehicle and sat between them looking like a Spanish grandee, immaculate in his white suit. Determined to be agreeable today, Sally said,

"You are the one who looks as though you came out of the nineteenth century. I understand that Mérida used to be called La Ciudad Blanca, because the residents always wore white, and the streets were so clean."

"They don't look any cleaner than anywhere else," sniffed Mary.

"And I don't see anyone else in white either," laughed Sally.

Maybe you are a throwback to another time." She turned to him with a broad smile.

"As far as conduct is concerned, my standards might be considered old-fashioned," he said priggishly.

Sally turned away from him. Why does he always have to get a dig in, harking back to his unpleasant behavior at Tenochtitlan, she wondered. Standards indeed! It's perfectly all right for him to put a hand on my thigh when it pleases him, or anything else he feels like doing. What a hypocrite he is! She added the last adjective to her growing list of things that she found offensive in Brian. Perhaps, if the list gets long enough, I can convince myself that I really dislike him and get him out of my life all together.

I really tried to be pleasant this morning, but with Miss Bitterness in the corner and Mr. Pain in the Neck on the other side, they have managed to spoil my mood. I'm going to stay out of their way if I can possibly manage.

After Teddy had told them where he wanted to have the photos set up, she stayed as close to him as possible.

He took pictures of the models in the carriages with some of the mansions as backdrops.

"I'm hungry," Sally announced, astounding herself in the process.

"What's come over you, Sarah? It used to be impossible to get you to eat, and now all you think about is food."

"It must be traveling that does it," she said.

"Travel is supposed to be broadening, maybe it will broaden you," said Brian.

Sally wrinkled her nose in disapproval of the pun.

"In any case," continued Brian, "it's a good thing for you to put on weight. You're much too thin. Women should look like women, not toothpicks. You have always been too thin."

"Always," Sally thought to herself. What does he mean by "always"? Does he know that Sarah is Sally? Does he really remember me? She glanced furtively at Brian who was carefully looking away from her.

"Mr. Lassiter, I'll eat when I'm hungry, not to please you, and I'm hungry now. The seafood is supposed to be wonderful here."

"That's true all over the Yucatan," said Brian, "but I do know that there's a wonderful seafood restaurant right on the Boulevard. They are famous for their oyster cocktail. Who's game to try?"

The tiny tiled restaurant open to the street was not particularly prepossessing, but the odors emanating were enough to stimulate even the most jaded of appetites. They all ordered a different cocktail - oysters, shrimps, crabs, and with the wonderful Mexican Beer it was enough to account for a whole meal.

"Do you think that you will be able to get anything good in the way of poses at Uxmal this afternoon? We've been dawdling all day." Brian asked Teddy.

"I don't think that we'll have a problem. It's really better to photograph in the later hours. The sun is so strong here and the light so harsh that mid-day is not the best time. By late afternoon we should be able to do better but early morning would be good as well. I prefer subtle light for shooting. Retouching is a nuisance and never as satisfying. I like to have it correct in the beginning."

Always professional in his approach to his work, Teddy was happy to discuss it with Brian and he, in turn, seemed interested in being on a businesslike basis with Teddy. He had spoken to him all day as though he were a respected partner in an important project.

"Do you know anything about the Sound and Light Show this evening? Will we be able to see it?" he asked.

"I don't see why not. We can stay at the Hotel at Uxmal tonight and do the shooting tomorrow morning."

After they arrived at Uxmal, Teddy began scouting around for good background shots. Almost anything I choose would be incredible. There is so much beauty here it is hard to believe that it is still intact after so long a time.

Uxmal is stunning. It was a place that the Mayas returned to at least five times. No one knows why they had left nor why they had returned or why it was finally abandoned. Their building skills were painstaking and exact. Beautiful geometric friezes were incorporated into the walls. Magnificent stone carvings of the rain-god "Chac" were part of the structure. The group wandered around, enraptured by the sights.

After darkness fell, seats were set up in the large quadrangle and the "Son et Lumiere Show" was to begin.

Brian whispered to Sally, sitting next to him.

"Every restored archeological site throughout the world puts on something like this, using tape recordings and spectacular lighting."

His hand rested on the back of her chair. She made no move to withdraw, as he had been perfectly pleasant all afternoon. I wish he would always behave like this, she thought to herself. Maybe I could find a new way to have a relationship with him if he were to behave like a person, not like someone who thinks that he owns me as well as everyone else in the world. Maybe it would be possible for him to have a relationship with a girl named Sarah. He seems to have forgotten that there ever was a girl named Sally. It's just as well. However, I seem unable to forget that there is a person named Brian. She wished that the arm dangling over the back of the chair so carelessly would suddenly enfold her to him. His strong masculine cologne blended with the soft scented night. She longed to touch him.

Suddenly the magnificent Mayan ruins were bathed in a bright yellow light as amplified sounds of Mayan music filled the air. The flutes and drums carried them back in time. The Sound and Light Show had begun. A fanciful story projected on the walls of the ruins was woven into the little known history of Uxmal as many colored lights spotlighted particular areas of architectural and historical interest. Although it was a synthetic experience, it was done well enough to have transported them back in time a thousand years.

Unconsciously Sally reached for Brian's hand as a particularly romantic story of a Mayan Prince and Princess was being told. It was only when the final sounds died down and the banal spotlights were turned on that she realized what she had done. She withdrew her hand as suddenly as though it had been burned and sat up straight in her chair, grateful for the cover of darkness hiding the blush on her cheeks.

The small plane swooped over the green-blue sea fringed by endless miles of white corals and beaches.

"I can't wait to get my feet into that sand," said Sally.

"Have you ever been on sand that was composed of ground coral?" Brian turned to speak to Sally.

"I don't know. What's the difference between that and any other beach? The only seashore I know has been Long Island and the New Jersey coast. I thought sand was sand."

Brian smiled. When he smiles like that, sweetly, without malice, his whole face lights up with beauty. His high cheekbones cause the piercing blue eyes to crinkle and shower sparks. Why can't he behave like this all the time, Sally wondered to herself.

"You need a resident tutor," he teased. "My poor little country mouse knows nothing about the real world, even something as simple as beaches."

There he goes again. Spoils it every time. Just when he makes me want to curl in his arms, he gets me so mad I could hit him.

Aloud she said, "Isn't it possible for you to speak to people pleasantly? You always sound as though you are at war with the world."

"Are you trying to teach me, you unsophisticated child?"

"You should listen to yourself sometimes. You sound like a pompous fool."

"Sally, shut up," whispered Teddy. "You'll ruin it."

Ignoring him, Sally continued facing Brian.

"Yes, I would like to know the difference. Could you explain it without sounding like a bore?"

"Coral sand is made of disintegrated coral. It is very fine and feels like talcum powder. The beaches that you know are decomposed rock and therefore are gritty. I think that the coral sand will please you. Did I explain that well? Was it simple enough? Too boring perhaps? Too pedantic? What grade would you give me?" He said sarcastically.

She didn't rise to the bait this time.

"Thank you," she said and turned about to face the window again.

They were landing at Playa de Carmen, a tiny town on the Caribbean coast of the Yucatan Peninsula.

"It is incredible," enthused Sally with glee. "It is a photographer's dream. There is no way that we can miss."

"Not true, Sarah," said Teddy. "It's very hard here because the light is so strong. Don't forget we're closer to the equator. I have to worry about glare. Again, I think we'd better wait to shoot until later this afternoon. This is a problem throughout this country. I told Brian that earlier."

"You see," Brian interposed, "even in your own field you have a great deal to learn."

"I don't mind asking questions and learning at all. It depends upon who is doing the teaching! Some people have a knack, and some don't." She turned on her heel, linking her arm in Teddy's.

"Come on, I'll race you down the beach! He's right about one thing. I never would believe that sand could be this soft. I can't wait to get into a bathing suit and cover myself with the sand and then run into the water."

"Run in is right. It looks as though you could walk for miles out there."

He pointed out to sea where the only people in view were still walking into the water, hundreds of feet out.

Suddenly, Sally panicked. How can I be on a beach and get into the water with make-up on. He'll see me and know who I am. Bravely she thought, what if he does. What difference does it make now. He's so rude to me anyway. I'm tired of this charade. Let whatever happens happen. I'm tired of worrying about him. He doesn't like me anyway. He just likes to get my goat whenever he can. He doesn't treat anyone else that way. I've only seen him being rude to Mary once or twice. I don't know why he feels that he has to pick on me. She remembered that last night she had reached for his hand at Uxmal. Embarrassed to think of it again, she also remembered that he had gently covered hers with his own. What am I to make of that? He never said a word, but afterwards when we walked through the ruins he held Mary's arm carefully so that she wouldn't trip on the uneven ground, not mine. She tossed her head impatiently.

"C'mon Teddy, I said 'let's race.'

They all explored the beach that afternoon. "It's fascinating, the jungle comes right down to the beach. We could be castaways on a deserted island; there's not a soul around here," Sally said.

"There are plenty of things in the jungle, but they're not human. This is a hunter's paradise. If you're willing and adventurous, which I'm sure Miss Unsophisticated will not be, we can eat rabbit, venison and muskrat. Don't, however, venture in without shoes. There are snakes, which are good eating too."

Brian said all of this with the obvious intention of shocking Sally. She wouldn't give him the satisfaction of seeming squeamish, but said aloud to Teddy,

"I have no objection to any food as long as it is cooked and seasoned well and, of course, served with the right wine.

"You can tell your assistant, Teddy," Brian said as they walked back to the plane, "that it's not just knowledge that counts, it's knowing where to apply it. The Yucatan is known for its beer. The beverage of choice here is beer."

He ostentatiously held her arm to help her back into the plane. It had been decided that they would fly up to Chichen Itza.

"There he goes again," Teddy whispered to Sally. "We're going to get a lecture on Chichen Itza."

They were walking together, arms around each other's waist. Teddy was so comforting thought Sally. He doesn't push me around as Brian does. He's a good friend even though I know that he would like it to be more than that. I wish that I could feel that way about him too; maybe I could get over this obsession that I have with Brian if I did. Aloud she said, "

It's not that I mind learning things. He certainly knows a lot and much of what he says is fascinating. It's his attitude. He thinks he's the only one who knows anything, that all of the rest of us are uneducated. He just gets on my nerves. It's a good thing that I never had a professor like him in school. I would never have finished college."

Sally and Teddy were walking ahead of the others when they heard Brian telling Mary loudly about the history of the archeological site.

"Well, it would be stupid not to find out what he has to say. I would like to know, and if we don't listen, the only one who loses out is us."

"True, but I hate to give him the satisfaction of our attention."

"That is cutting off your nose to spite your face, isn't it?"

"I suppose so," agreed Sally, "but," and she gritted her teeth, "he's so annoying." However, she and Teddy waited for the others to catch up so that they could hear what Brian was saying.

"That pyramid in front of you is an example of the astronomical genius of the Mayas. Look at the main staircase. It's 78 feet high." He pointed at the broad shallow steps that rose up the face of the edifice.

"Can you see the carved serpent head at the base? Now notice that the staircase projects outward from the pyramid which is really a series of stepped back terraces. Can you imagine that on March 21 and September 21, the spring and fall equinoxes, the sun casts shadows on the face of the pyramid which connect to the carved serpent head at the base, so that it looks as though there is a huge serpent coming down from the temple at the top. Only on those two days of the year does the shadow form an entire serpent. Not only that, the arithmetic that went into the planning of the building is unbelievable. Each of the stairways on all four sides of the pyramid have 91 steps; adding the step to the summit makes 365."

"The days of the year," said Mary.

"It's amazing, especially since there doesn't seem to have been contact with any European cultures. They designed an accurate calendar as well."

"Now I want to show you the famous basketball court." They followed Brian, impressed in spite of themselves by his seemingly inexhaustible fund of knowledge. He led them to a large field almost 300 feet long bounded by two walls 200 feet apart in which two stone rings were imbedded. The walls were covered with carved stone panels depicting a game which looked as though it could be basketball.

"The story, as portrayed in the stone, seems to have been that the losers were sacrificed to the gods," he explained.

"Do you think that's where the expression 'sudden death' comes from," joked Teddy?

"You mean in football?"

"Very funny," said Sally sarcastically.

"Anyway," continued Brian, "the other thing that is fascinating about the court is that its acoustics are so perfect that if you whisper even to yourself you can be heard at the other end of the court."

He wandered away by himself to study the carvings in the wall. It was as though he had finished his lecture and wanted to be alone. The others, too, were wandering around the court by themselves trying to decipher the ancient carvings, when over the still air was heard "I WILL NOT SHARE HER."

Everyone froze just where they were. The sound was sepulchral, disembodied as it was. It was as though the whispered cry had been wrenched from someone's depths. No one knew who had uttered the pained whisper.

They had flown to Cancun, the resort that the Mexican government had created out of a sand strip. Magnificent hotel after magnificent hotel had been built along the coast to rival the best of the world's seaside playgrounds. Mary had made reservations in the most luxurious of all. Every sport other than mountain climbing, skiing and ice skating was available.

Sally had come down to the pool dressed in a bikini. She wore the matching jacket as she was not too comfortable with the immodesty of the suit. Her face was clean of make-up and her hair pulled back into a pony tail. She was sitting at a table drinking club soda when Brian appeared. He had purchased some guayaberras, those marvelous Mexican shirts which replaced jackets in this humid hot climate. His was a light blue that played up the color of his eyes, embroidered in the front with a darker blue thread. The last few days had turned his normally swarthy skin into a deep tan which enhanced the brilliance of his deep blue eyes, while his black moustache contrasted with the white of his teeth. Sally was looking out toward the ocean and did not see him coming. However, there was not a woman seated there who was not struck by his compelling looks. It was with envy that they saw him headed toward the table where the beautiful redhead was seated.

He did not take his eyes off Sally from the moment he arrived at the pool area. Neither the pool, the ocean, nor the beach had any interest for him.

"May I join you?"

"Of course, if you're pleasant."

Her hand flew to her mouth as she realized that this was the first time that he had seen her without any make-up

The waiter came to the table for his order.

"Have you tried the Margaritas here? They're excellent. Oh, I forgot. You don't care for liquor."

To the man he said,

"One Margarita and one club soda." Turning toward Sally, "It's about time you came out from that mask. What were you hiding from? Beautiful women don't need all of that stuff on their faces."

She stared at him open-mouthed. Had he known her all of the time, or was it possible that he had forgotten that afternoon at his apartment. She determined to carry this off as a sophisticated woman, trying to forget what had happened before just as he seemed to have forgotten.

"It's too hot," she answered shortly, rose suddenly, took off her jacket and dived into the cool refreshing water.

She swam many lengths of the pool back and forth until she felt more at ease. Then she turned on her back and floated until her adrenalin settled down so that she could face Brian calmly. I wish I knew how to handle this man. Sometimes I think that he hates me, and sometimes I think that he likes me. I also wish I knew what I felt about him. At times I wish that I could rake his face with my nails and hurt him as much as he hurts me, and other times I wish that he would hold me tightly and make love to me in the way that I know that he can, in the way that he started to that awful day. I would like to be with him forever. Startled by this admission to herself, she began to backstroke rapidly, unaware of the nearness of the edge of the pool, she slammed her head into the coping. Abruptly she felt two hands under her arms pull her out of the water.

"You are not to be trusted at all. I keep telling you that you need a tutor. I think perhaps a nanny would be more appropriate."

Resentfully she turned to look at her savior. Brian's Guayaberra was soaking wet from her dripping body, showing the black curly hairs on his chest.

"I was perfectly all right. I was enjoying myself. What gave you the right to decide that I should come out of the pool? You do not own me!" At that she pulled away and took one step forward. Swaying from side to side she put her hand to her head.

"Let me feel." He forced her chin up and at the time felt the top of her head. He whistled to himself, "That's a nasty bump. Come with me and we'll put something cold on it."

He firmly held her hand and steered her toward the table where he helped her to sit down.

Mary had arrived carrying a bottle of beer.

"Let me have that beer, Mary." He took Mary's unopened bottle and pressed the ice cold glass against Sally's head. She attempted to force his hands away.

"Stop that, you idiot." He brushed her hands down as though they were merely annoying insects.

"Oh, that hurts. Stop pressing that thing against my head."

"If I don't, you're going to have one swelled head very soon."

"That wouldn't be much of a change, she generally does."

This came from Mary, who was now sitting sullenly at the table.

"Unworthy, you cat. Are you jealous of a bottle of beer?"

"Jealous? Certainly not. I was just commenting on the fact that your mermaid thinks she knows everything about everything. She knows that Brian can fix everything. Isn't that so, Brian?" She added maliciously, "I would contribute my bottle of beer anytime to the young lady's well being." She called the waiter for another beer and some ice as well.

Brian meanwhile was forcing the bottle against the rapidly

swelling lump on Sally's head, while she was protesting and wriggling to get away from him. It was at this moment that Teddy came down to the poolside with his ever present cameras. He had been at the bar and had had more than one Margarita before he discovered that the others were outside.

"What are you doing Brian? Is that the way you subdue your women these days? That's rather a primitive approach more suited for the jungle than such an elegant spot as this. Somehow I never figured you to be a caveman type."

His speech was a bit slower than usual as it was apparent that he was not quite sober. Normally he wouldn't have had the nerve to challenge Brian about anything, but the alcohol gave him false courage.

"Wow, Sal, um I mean Sarah, that's quite a suit. Or should I say non-suit. There's sure not much of it. Is there Mary?"

Mary looked at Teddy with disdain. "I guess it's all right if you like that sort of thing. I can't imagine that it would be good for long distance swimming."

"What's going on here, anyway. I seem to have walked into something."

"Nothing at all," answered Mary silkily. "Your girl friend cracked her head on the edge of the pool carelessly, and 'our hero' is making it all better."

"Oh Sal, are you all right?" asked Teddy worriedly.

"She's fine, she just needs a keeper, poor thing," said Brian. "I don't think that you are man enough for the job, Ted. I think that I have to fire you as Sarah's, I mean Sally's, protector."

Sally, infuriated by the conversation which seemed to have her as its butt, forced Brian's hands away and stood up.

"I'm fine now. Leave me alone all of you."

She was so angry that she never thought to put on her jacket and the three at the table watched her storm furiously away. The beauty of her firm young body with its long lean legs and slim torso, topped by the riotous flame of her hair, caught everyone's eye as she left.

Sally's head ached for a while and then she discovered that the bump was still there but much smaller. What a fuss over nothing! You'd think I had killed myself the way Brian behaved. And that Mary! What a spiteful cat! She can't stand to have Brian pay any attention to anyone. In spite of herself, Sally was pleased at Mary's annoyance and Brian's solicitude. She had liked the feel of leaning against his hard-muscled body while she was dizzy. Amusedly she remembered how soaked his shirt was. That's twice now I've gotten him soaking wet. But this time I didn't mean it. I wish I knew that he liked me. I think I'm just a diversion for him. He's probably bored with us down here. I know he cares for Mary, but I think she's too possessive for him. If he can't be showing off, or behaving like a big shot, he teases me. It must be because none of us is exciting enough for him. I wonder what kind of a woman he really would like. I wonder why he never married. She fell asleep dreaming of what it would be like if Brian were holding her right now. She had the recurring dream of the afternoon in his apartment, but it didn't end with Hank's calling her. Now she heard the words, "I won't share her," and then the telephone shattered her awake.

"Sally."

"Uh huh."

"SALLY," Brian shouted. "Get up and talk to me."

"What! What's wrong?"

"Are you awake?"

"Yes-yes, what do you want?" she answered angrily. "You woke me! You can hear that I'm awake. Can I have no peace from you?"

"I just wanted to make sure that you are all right. I - Oh, never mind." She heard the phone slam down hard.

Looking at the clock she realized that she could not have been sleeping for more than an hour. Stretching, she went into the bathroom to shower and wash her hair. Chlorine smells so I feel as though I been through the wash cycle. What the devil is wrong with that man. He thinks he owns all of us. I'll be glad when this assignment is over and I can go back to a normal life. Suddenly the thought of that unknown normal life stretched in front of her unappealingly. It was fun working with Teddy, but she knew too that she would miss the ongoing battle with Brian. No, it's not the battle that I miss. I wish that we didn't fight all of the time. I just want to be with him if he were to behave as he did when we first met.

Angrily she scrubbed her scalp, wincing as she touched the remains of the bump. She was toweling herself dry, when she heard the knock at the door. Wrapping the towel around her hair and another around her body, she went to answer it.

"Who is it?"

"The big bad wolf!" said Brian's voice.

Unthinkingly she opened the door. As he entered she remembered that she had practically nothing on.

He saw the blush rise to her cheeks.

"Stop worrying, you have more covering now than you did with those ridiculous strips of cloth this afternoon. Besides I only came to feel your head, not the rest of your anatomy."

Her face flamed to match her hair; she stood saying nothing.

"What? No retort. What's happened to you, Sally-Sarah? Have you lost your tongue?"

Unbidden tears welled up and rolled down her cheeks. Brian reached forward to pull her into his arms. Holding her gently, he murmured,

"I really was afraid of concussion. If you hit your head as hard as I think you did, you can't be allowed to sleep too long. I came to check you. Open your eyes, you silly, and let me see your pupils."

Abashed at her show of emotion, and sure that he just didn't want a member of his crew to cause him problems by being injured, she pulled away from him.

"Teddy could have done that for me."

"Teddy had a hard time finding the door to his own room. You certainly don't choose your men very well. First Hank and now Teddy."

"Hank - what do you mean Hank?"

"Come on Sally, I've known you were the girl in the park and in MY BEDROOM all of this time. I just don't understand what it is in these men that attracts you to them. As I said my dear, your taste needs cultivating. You're just a small town girl."

"You're not the one to teach me." She pushed him away. "Go take care of Mary. She's the one who needs you. I don't."

Coldly he turned from her.

"Very well. Please be ready for dinner at 8:30. We plan to meet in the lobby and then we're going to a disco here. Does that meet with your majesty's approval?" He bowed mockingly from the waist.

"I'll be ready."

And she was. She didn't feel like dressing up tonight. She was angry at herself and angry at Brian. No matter what, they seemed to leave each other unpleasantly. So she just wore tight jeans and a plain tee shirt and wrapped a green ribbon around her hair to keep it out of her eyes and absolutely no make-up. She looked years younger than she ever had before.

Brian raised an eyebrow at her appearance, but made no comment. Mary, of course, was dressed smartly in a barebacked full-skirted blue dress, showing off her trim figure. Brian ostentatiously offered her his arm as they went into dinner, while Teddy and Sally followed with the others. Brian paid no attention to anyone other than Mary during dinner and Mary preened herself like a cat. Sally deliberately paid attention to Teddy and listened to the experiences of the other models who had spent the day at the artisans' market.

After dinner they took a cab to the best disco in town (according to the maitre d'). Sally threw herself into dancing with abandon.

"It's not possible to believe that she had such a nasty crack on the head earlier in the day," Mary commented on her wild dancing.

"Men apparently turn her on, they seem to mend all wounds." she added snidely as one partner after the other selected her to dance with them.

Brian abruptly turned his back on the disco floor. Throwing down a fistful of pesos he said coldly as he got up,

"Teddy, you pay for everything. Mary and I are, leaving. I would like to get an early start over to Cozumel tomorrow so don't make it too late a night."

Before Sally fell asleep that night she tossed and turned and thoughts washed over her. She couldn't remember all of the men that had danced with her. She only knew that she had wanted to dance with Brian, but he had disappeared with Mary. That Mary! So cool and sophisticated. I hate her. Never a hair out of place, always perfectly and appropriately dressed. She knew that her own outfit last night had angered Brian. She had known that it would and that was why she had deliberately chosen it. I wonder whom I hate more, Mary or Brian. As she realized the question that she had asked herself, she burst into laughter. Who am I kidding, she wondered. If I didn't love Brian, I wouldn't hate Mary, so I guess I must love Brian. But why is he such an awful person? Sanctimonious, Inconsiderate, Rude, Condescending, Cruel, Spoiled, Nasty-tempered, Bossy, Blue-eyed, Steely blue-eyed, Artic blue-eyed, Midnight blue-eyed, Piercing blue-eyed, Magnetic blue-eyed. Everytime he looks at me I absolutely dissolve. Why can't he love me? If he only loved me, I could love him so hard. I do anyway, but he will never know it. I hate him and I hate Mary. I wonder where they went last night when they left the disco. I don't want to know. Yes, I want to know. Is she his mistress?

"Oh Brian," she murmured aloud as she embraced her pillow tightly,

"I need you." She fell asleep dreaming about the feel of his body as he had held her close when he pulled her out of the pool, his lean muscular strength supporting her.

"I must say you look a wreck, Sally." Brian greeted Sally with these words as she climbed into the plane that was to fly them on the short hop aver to Cozumel.

"Don't you think that it's rather irresponsible to stay out all night when you have work to do this morning? This is a job, you know."

"Thank you," she retorted coldly in kind.

"I am perfectly capable of doing whatever it is that Teddy requires of me." She buckled herself into her seat and faced the window so as to discourage further conversation. She was grateful for the dark glasses that curtained her eyes from the insistent sun. The glare of the beaches and the brightness of the water was hard to take for someone who had slept so little last night. Fortunately the flight was short enough to discourage conversation.

As THEY DROVE AROUND THE island in a rented jeep, the beauty and charm caused Sally to say,

"I wish that we could come back here just to swim and snorkel, I have never seen such water."

"It's true," said Teddy, "they say that some of the best snorkeling is right here on the Palancar reef."

"How long do you think that we'll have to be here, Teddy, I mean for the shots that you need."

"Well, it's up to Brian, really. I don't know how many shots at the beach he wants."

"It's really not up to Brian at all," Sally replied indignantly. "This was supposed to be Hank's project."

She tapped Brian on the shoulder, "What happened to Hank? I thought that he was going to meet us down here and finish what he started."

Brian tightened his grip on the wheel. "Finish what he started? Yes, I guess you would like that wouldn't you?"

"Of course, I would like that. I think that people have the right to have the satisfaction of finishing what they start. Why isn't he here?"

Ignoring her question he asked,

"Isn't one man enough for you? Or isn't Teddy doing his job well?

"His job well? Of course he always does. He's the best around."

"Oh really?" He could hardly be heard over the roar of the motor. "I always said that you were unsophisticated."

Disgustedly Sally turned to Teddy. "He's in a foul mood this morning. He's talking in riddles. I don't understand what he's saying. You talk to me. He makes me sick."

Teddy put his arm around her.

"Don't let him get to you, honey. It's so beautiful here. Forget him and look at those beaches."

They had driven around the island to the Caribbean side, where the road stretched endlessly without sign of any habitation except for a flock of noisy parrots chattering loudly as they flew above.

"Is there anything here that you want to shoot, Teddy, since you are the artistic director of this expedition?" Brian shouted.

" I think so, but I think that I'd like to get into the village, perhaps that would be a better background. I hope that we can do justice to the sea and the incredible beauty of the sand."

"Could we come back after lunch and do some snorkeling, do you think," asked Sally of Teddy. "Ask him, you know, ask the king! I don't want to talk to him at all," she spoke quietly to Teddy.

"Let's wait until we have lunch back in town. We have to rent the equipment there anyway, or get a boat. I think that we have to go to the other side of the island to the reef to be able to do it."

They drove back to the center of Cozumel. It had been a simple fishing village until about thirty years ago, when it had been discovered by divers and snorkelers. The town square had been modernized but it was still the place where all of the villagers congregated. As the weather was never inclement, every night everyone came to town, babies and all, and sat around the plaza where there were a number of good restaurants and dive shops as well. Teddy planned some shots for the models in the square and then wondered if they might try some snorkeling after they had a bite to eat.

"Have any of you ever snorkled? asked Brian.

"No, but I'm sure that you have and can teach us," said Sally, a bit sarcastically.

"Did you bring a bathing suit or that ridiculous piece of nothing that you were wearing yesterday?"

Sally ignored him as they walked over to the dive shop. They were able to rent a boat with a captain and all of the equipment necessary to snorkel for the afternoon.

The island was even more beautiful when seen from the ocean. The clarity of the air and the water was indescribable. Looking down from the boat they were able to see huge schools of fish lazily swimming by.

The crystal clear ocean was irresistible. Sally impatiently listened to the rather simple instructions that were necessary for the snorkeling.

She let herself down the ladder into the warm sea. Never having worn a mask before she was surprised at the ability to see so clearly under water. Astoundingly the fish seemed unafraid and had no hesitation in swimming right up to her face, their colors amazingly bright. The green and blue angelfish ranging in size from an inch or two up to two feet swam placidly by as though she were not there. Suddenly a curtain of tiny fish appeared from nowhere. They hung suspended in front of her until she made a sudden movement and they turned as one organism and darted away. The intense blue of some of the fish looked as though it couldn't be real, it was so deep a color.

She found herself swimming next to Brian who took hold of her wrist and pulled her alongside. She struggled to pull away but then saw that he was pointing to something in the coral reef. He pointed out a tiny moray eel, its head just coming out of its cave. Brian teased it with a piece of coral and the little eel opened his mouth in anger. Brian pantomimed that he wasn't to be played with and she realized that those little teeth were sharp indeed. They swam slowly, propelled by the effortless kicking of their fins.

It was not necessary to use their arms to go forward and Brian held Sally's hand as they explored the beauty of the sea. He had attached to his wrist a waterproof guide to the fish and corals of the area and together they looked for the pictures of the beauties of the underwater scene and identified the coral and the fish. She loved the little damselfish whose brilliant electric blue spots on the body reminded her of Brian's eyes. The parrot fish astounded her as large four-foot specimens striped in reds and greens floated by, unconcerned at their presence. It was a whole new world under water. He carefully pointed out the stinging coral that could burn if she were to touch it. It was with great reluctance that she followed Brian back to the boat.

"I have never enjoyed anything as much as that," she said as she pulled herself aboard. She pushed her wet hair back, her eyes sparkling with the enjoyment of a new discovery.

"There's a whole universe! I have never seen such colors. The shapes and colors of the coral are magnificent."

She stood up, moving aside so that Brian could climb up. Her wet lithe body shone in the sunlight. Her skin, tanned by the strong Mexican sun made her seen like a bronze goddess risen from the sea.

Sheets of water cascaded down Brian's body as he hoisted himself into the boat. Rivulets ran through the coarse hair on his chest while the sheen of the water accented all of his muscles. His lean body was beautiful. It was really the first time that Sally had seen him in a bathing suit. I didn't realize, she thought, he's even more handsome than I imagined. Aloud she said,

"That was wonderful. I loved it! I can't wait to do it again."

Leaning against the railing of the boat, She and Brian were alone at the stern, the others having gone up on the top deck. She was fanning her long red hair out to dry in the breeze, as the sun shimmered off her golden skin. She was unaware of her graceful beauty as she toweled herself dry.

"This towel is drenched," she laughed, "throw me another, will you." Somehow it all seemed so easy now. He handed her a towel that rapidly became a turban as she wound it around her streaming hair. Brian, already dried, gazed at her as she lounged against the seat, arms clasped around one knee, staring peacefully out to sea.

"I feel so wonderful. There can be nothing like swimming in a warm ocean to make you feel as though everything is right with the world. My body feels good, my mind is relaxed, and I can't get over the beautiful sights beneath the water." She stretched lazily and continued,

"I think that I have died and gone to heaven." Then turning to face him she smiled, a brilliant smile, the double dimple becoming a deep line in her cheek and the warm brown eyes reflecting her contentedness.

There was no tension between them; there was no friction. It was as though they were really good, comfortable friends.

"That's quite a chapeau you have," Brian teased. "It must be quite the latest style."

"Why yes," she answered in kind. "I thought I might wear it for dinner tonight. Perhaps I could pin a ruby in front to show off my jewels."

"No, no, not a ruby. It wouldn't go with your hair. An emerald. That's it, an emerald. It would complement your coloring. I must have one around here, somewhere."

"Now, what do you think of this?" She grabbed an orange life jacket and put it on.

"How is this for a top to my evening gown?" She leaned back parodying a model's stance.

"Marvelous, it does wonders for your figure. You look so svelte. I knew that you had been eating a lot on this trip, but I hadn't thought you had gained quite that much weight."

"Now you, let me fix you up." She took another towel and swathed his head in it making him look like a ravishing rajah. His blue eyes shone out from his tanned skin enhanced by the whiteness of the towel.

"For you, oh sir," she mockingly bowed, "I will lend my second best sapphire, to match your eyes."

"Second best! I am entitled to your first best!"

"Oh no," she teased, "you have to earn that. Let me fix your pants."

"My pants! You shock me, Miss Harte."

Sally had taken another towel, knelt down and was draping it around his narrow waist. At the touch of her cool hand on his warm skin Brian put his hand on her head and pressed her to his body. Shocked at the contact she stumbled to her feet, and covered her mouth with her hands.

"You can't bear to touch me," can you, Sally? "Only others!" He pushed her away from him and tore up the stairs to the deck above.

She reeled back in surprise. She didn't understand what had happened. They had been having fun for the first time. It had been such a beautiful afternoon. There had been an ease and camaraderie between them, and then suddenly he spoiled it all. What had she done, just moved back because she was afraid to give into herself. She had longed to put her arms around his waist and hold him to her. She had found herself wanting him to hold her tightly. Their physical proximity and their repartee they had made her feel so close to him, and then the shock of their contact had made her pull back afraid - but afraid of her own desire. And then his precipitous withdrawal. Why did he turn everything into something ugly? What did he mean "others"? It's no good between us. There can be no meeting ground. Nothing is ever right. He's hateful. He must hate me. He taunts me, ridicules me. That whole scene was only to make fun of me. I thought that we were having a good time, but evidently he didn't think so. Yet he can be kind and gentle. Swimming with him was fun. I don't know what to make of him. Any time I let down my guard, he hurts me. I wish this trip were over.

Teddy came clattering down the stairs.

"That's a ridiculous outfit you have on. I got a few shots of you from above. I thought you would like to have a record of what you looked like today."

Angrily she unwound the turban and took off the jacket and threw them on the bench.

"What's the matter, babe? Did you have a fight with Mr. High and Mighty? He came storming up the stairs, spoke to the captain, but wouldn't talk to anyone else, just grunted when Mary asked him a question. I hope that you don't make him so mad that he cuts the trip. I can't understand why you try to get at him all of the time. He's the boss of the whole shebang. This campaign will go down the tubes if he decides to do it in. Why can't you be nice to him? I know he's difficult, but you have to put up with some unpleasantness in business. Don't fret now."

Teddy sat next to Sally and put his arm around her shoulder. His warm concern for her triggered the unhappy tears that slid down her golden cheeks. Fiercely she said to herself, I will not cry for him. I will not let him make me cry. Angrily she brushed away the tears and threw her arm around Teddy, much to his surprise and delight.

"Thank you for always being kind, Teddy." She kissed his cheek and went in to change her clothes.

Brian, on his way down to do the same, saw Sally embracing Teddy. Too far away to hear any of the conversation, he drew his own conclusions.

"Slut," he murmured to himself.

Mary had booked the group into a suite at the newest of the hotels on the island. A duplex with four rooms upstairs, a communal living room and two other bedrooms downstairs, it opened onto its own private patio which in turn led to the soft coral sands leading to the glistening sea. It was furnished luxuriously with comfortable couches and chairs, a bar, stocked with every alcoholic beverage imaginable, and a small refrigerator held ice, wine and beer and different soft drinks. Picking up the colors of the inviting living room handsome prints of Mexican life were hung on the walls. As here were few people at the hotel it was as though they had their own private beach all to themselves.

After everyone had showered and dressed for the evening, Brian entered the living room, with Mary close behind.

"Please make your own arrangements for dinner this evening. Too much togetherness is not such a good thing."

"I couldn't agree more," said Mary and smiled satisfiedly. She put her arm on his arm possessively.

"You can eat at the hotel if you like, or if you choose, rent a car and go to town and just charge it to the room. Go ahead." He held the door open for her.

"Wow! What got into him?" Teddy asked of no one in particular after they left.

"I'm delighted," said Sally. "We don't have to have his black presence hovering over us tonight. Let's go down to the lobby and find out what is happening where. Then we can go into town. There are lots of restaurants, and there's dancing. It looks like fun. I can't wait to see the square at night. That's when the whole village comes out I was told.

"Do you want to come with us?" she asked the others.

Sally deliberately forced herself into a lively mood. Left to her own devices she would happily have climbed into bed and mourned for her lost love. I won't allow myself to behave that way. I have got to pull myself out of this. I can't respond to him so self-destructively. I will not! I am going to have F U N. Pulling at Teddy, she said,

"Come on."

The others decided to see what the hotel was like for dinner, but thought that they might come into town later on. So Teddy and Sally rented a car and drove into town. The square was ablaze with lights and the Mexican children were as active as though it were the middle of the day. Parents were sitting on benches and talking, holding infants or carrying them around with them as they walked. Most of the shops were opened. It was a lively exciting place, where everyone seemed good-humored. They decided to walk around the square, stopping at all of the restaurants and looking at the menus posted in the window, wandering from place to place and innocently holding hands like good friends do. Teddy was so comfortable, thought Sally, for the nine hundredth time. If only he doesn't want any more than being my friend, we will be able to work together well.

She was resolved to forget Brian and wished that the trip were over. I can get back to my job modeling for Teddy for a while, and then I think that I am going to just save up my money. I can't go back to that store, but I do want to get into a job that's challenging. Maybe I'll leave New York. There's nothing to hold me there. Aunt Helen wants to go. I can go with her. I'd like to try some place new. This trip has opened my eyes. It's a big world. I'll model for a year, save money and then travel with the wind. Footloose and fancy-free! That will be me. Maybe I'll even go back to school and get an advanced degree.

"Sally! Listen, I've been talking to you for ten minutes and you are definitely not here. Where are you? Day dreaming?"

"I guess so." Her thoughts about the future would just have to wait.

"I guess I was, Teddy, sorry." She wasn't ready to share them with Teddy just yet. She forced herself back into the present. They stopped outside a restaurant separated only by a railing from the plaza. It was full of people happily eating.

"This looks good here, Teddy. You like lobster, don't you?"

"Who doesn't, and look they have something called lemon soup. Let's go in."

They entered the open restaurant and were shown to a table.

"Look, half of the menu is in English," she laughed. "I like it better when it's all in Spanish. I feel as though it's more authentic."

"True, but this place really exists on tourism. With such wonderful scuba and snorkeling places, many folks from the States come down."

When he waiter came they agreed on the lemon soup and lobster and potatoes. When it came, Sally said,

"I'll never be able to eat it all."

"Do you want to bet? Your appetite has improved and swimming always makes me hungry. Doesn't it do that to you?"

She attacked the lobster with gusto after the soup, the waiter nodding in approval. He was unable to keep his eyes off Sally, every time he passed her table. She had lobster all over her, her face was covered and there was lobster in her hair.

"I think I need a bath," she laughed.

"Postres ,cafe?" The waiter hovered near.

"Postres? Oh dessert? Teddy, how about dessert?"

"Can you eat any more, Sally?"

"No," she said regretfully. "I really can't. I think just coffee for me. I couldn't even finish those delicious potatoes. What were they?"

"Just potatoes cut thin and fried," said Teddy. "I couldn't finish either."

"Dos cafes, por favor," he said to the waiter. "I don't think I have ever eaten so much. But it was marvelous."

Unseen by them, Brian and Mary had passed the open restaurant and observed the two.

"They certainly seem to get along well together," Mary commented.

"Since they work together, I guess they had better," Brian replied.

"Come now, don't you think that there's more to it than that," she said tauntingly?

"I really wouldn't know, Mary, and what's more, I really don't care," he said icily.

Just then Sally and Teddy burst into laughter as Sally was showing him the mess that she had made of her meal. Brian glared at them as they passed. An observer would have wondered what the beautiful red head had ever done to warrant such anger.

The next morning Sally got up early to go for a swim. She went alone because no one else was up, and felt that the water was so calm she would have no problems. Even though, she heard Aunt Helen's voice in the back of her mind,

"Never, never swim alone. You know that anyone, even the very best swimmer, can get cramps and drown. Promise me Sally."

"But," she answered her aunt silently, "that was the Jersey shore you were talking about. And that was the time before flippers, masks and snorkels. I'm going where it's close to shore and I can always grab onto the coral." Having convinced herself that she would be quite all right, she took the rented equipment and walked down to the water.

The pristine white powder stretched to the horizon while the early morning light glanced off the turquoise water and bounced back into the azure sky. She felt as though she were the only occupant of an enchanted isle. The palm trees swayed in the breeze and the flocks of tiny parrots advanced and retreated, swooping around suddenly and chattering madly as they flew. This must be heaven, she thought, as the breeze gently ruffled her hair and caressed her skin. I wish that I could stay here forever. Thoughts of Brian fleetingly entered and left, leaving her momentarily uneasy. Quickly, she forced them away and concentrated on her physical awareness of the beach and its beauty.

She waded into the water and sat down in the shallows. After wetting her mask by spitting into it as she had been taught, and placing it on her face, she donned the flippers and proceeded to walk out until the water had reached her waist. She then stretched out and began to swim around the reef. Keeping her head below the surface with the snorkel above so that she could breathe she was able to see clearly at the sea bottom as the visibility was so good. Entranced by the colors and shapes of the coral she followed the contours of the reef, totally unaware of its relationship to the beach that she had left. She was more interested in the coral of the reef since there were few fish in evidence. I should have brought some food to attract them I guess, but it doesn't matter, the reef is wonderful as well, with incredible growths of live coral. She kicked lazily, putting more and more distance between her position and the hotel. Entranced by the rise and fall of the sea floor and luxuriating in the sensuous feel of the water, she felt suspended in time. She was interested in the reef's formations. I wish that I knew more about the sea life, she thought. The colors and variety of form are fascinating. She passed tall brown growths that looked like branches of trees, and then round collections that seemed to be bunches of green flowers, tall swaying purple and green sheets that could easily have been fans undulating in response to the movement of the ocean.

There were caves that she wanted to explore, but remembered the pretty little moray eel with the sharp little teeth and decided that she would keep her hands away. I wish that I had gloves, though, she thought. After awhile she lifted her head to see where she was. She looked toward the beach and saw nothing but a long empty stretch of sand. She then realized that the current had helped her to cover a tremendous distance. I had better go back, she thought.

She turned in the other direction. I have no idea how far I have been carried, nor do I know how long I've been out. I had better get back before I'm missed or Teddy will worry. She put her head down and started to swim. She was working hard, grateful for the aid of the flippers. It had been so easy coming down, but it was a struggle to get back. The shore seemed so far away. I wish I were on that other beach, the first one that we saw. I could walk back, but looking down she realized that this coral reef was very deep. She was going to have to swim all the way and fight the current as she did so.

The beauty of the bottom of the sea palled as she became interested only in retracing her journey. She seemed to be making no headway. What had been so easy to do became more and more difficult as she kicked. The fins that had seemed such help before, acquired a weight of their own. It was becoming harder to move her legs. The one thing that I know I must not do is to panic. I have to keep calm and work steadily, keep moving my legs up and down, up and down. She began to pull with her arms as well and seemed to move a bit faster. She was aware of her snail-like progress as she kept watching the sea bed. Clumps of coral that had been ahead of her, slowly, oh so slowly, moved behind her as she crawled along. Now and then she raised her head to see the shoreline. It would be horrible if she were to be swimming away from shore. Although she was trying to swim diagonally, she found that she constantly had to correct her course. If I stop and rest, I'll just be pulled down to the place I started from, since the current is so strong. I must keep going. No longer interested in the bottom except as a guide to her progress, she did not see the huge parrot fish that came up from underneath. It turned to confront her, just slightly curious as to what she was doing there. The expression of imperturbability on its face made her laugh aloud. In doing so she broke the seal of her mask and it began to fill with water. She began thrashing her legs to help her tread water so that she could rise above it and empty her mask. Forcing herself up took a great deal of energy. I can't make it, she thought. I have to get into shore, but it seems so far away. Clearing her mask she put it back again and swam toward the shore, no longer trying to take a diagonal course. I can walk back to the hotel, if I can ever reach the beach. Suddenly, the placid sea had become an inhospitable, alien and unforgiving environment. Oh, Aunt Helen, you generally are right. Why didn't I listen to your advice? Ploddingly she continued, stroking and kicking. Fleetingly she thought of Brian. If I don't make it, my one regret will be that Brian and I could never establish a decent relationship. Oh, how I wish he were here. Imagining that he were there made her angry, in that she was sure that the first thing that he would say would be something like, "No one can leave you on your own at all. You need a Nanny. First pyramid climbing, now swimming alone! How can an intelligent woman behave so stupidly?" Knowing what he would say infuriated her so that she was flooded by a jolt of adrenalin. I will get back and I'm going to do it by myself! I can do it! I will do it! I must do it or else I'm a goner because there's no one else around, she thought. Her final surge of energy brought her up to a coral reef close to the shore. Reaching for the ledge, she pulled herself forward, too tired to keep swimming. Finally, she found a passage that led to the beach and gratefully she tumbled out of the water and lay prostrate on the sand.

"Red headed mermaids. I've never seen a red-haired mermaid.

The only ladies of that ilk I have known always had long dark hair and they sit on rocks and play the harp. This is a different variety. I wonder if it, or rather she, speaks English."

From a distance, Sally heard the taunting words. Slowly she raised her head to see a tanned foot and a well-shaped leg. Too tired to get up, she allowed her head to drop back onto the soft sand.

"Sally, what's wrong?"

She felt her arm grabbed and a strong finger placed on the wrist.

"Speak to me, you impossible wench! I can't leave you out of my sight for a minute." Then after a moment of silence,

"Your pulse is all right," he said in relief.

Brian continued,

"You've been swimming alone! How far did you go? You have absolutely no sense! Are you all right? Say something, damn it!"

"Tired, I'm so tired," she sighed, letting her head droop against his chest. It was so comfortable. She felt safe where she was. She tried to raise her arms, but they fell back. For once Brian said nothing. He just held her and rocked her gently, occasionally smoothing her hair back from her face. She lay there with her eyes closed, exhausted but content.

His strong arms lifted her up and carried her down the beach the rest of the distance to the hotel. Hardly aware of anything but the security that she felt she was satisfied to stay as she was forever. She fell asleep and dreamed that Brian was holding her tightly and telling her that he would never let her go.

When Sally awakened she didn't know where she was. She had slept deeply with no idea of the time passing. She tried to sit up but found that her arms were leaden. Remembering then the morning's experience, she groaned aloud at her stupidity. Everyone knows that swimming alone is absolutely forbidden. It's the first rule of water safety. How could I have been such an idiot!

The door opened and a tall figure was silhouetted against the light from the living room.

"Are you up? Do you feel all right? Oh, you are a foolish girl. How could you have gone out alone? What happened?"

He pulled back the drapes at the windows, causing her to cover her eyes against the light.

In spite of the scolding words, the concern in Brian's voice was evident. Luxuriating in his apparent anxiety about her well-being, she said in a small voice,

"The beach was so seductive this morning. The water so welcoming, I couldn't resist going in. No one else was up, so I went alone."

Brian walked over to the bed and sat on its edge, then lifted her small hand and held it in his.

"You are such a foolish child. You need..."

"A Nanny," she chimed in and giggled. "Sometimes I think that you are right. I knew that you would say that to me. As a matter of fact that knowledge made me so angry that it gave me the extra strength to get to shore. You really are horrid to me, you know."

He slipped his arm behind her and raised her up against the pillows.

"Horrid to you? I wonder. I don't think so. You are a maddening little person. Just look at the idiotic things you do. The last adventure was when you cracked your head. How do you feel now? Would you like something to drink? Thank goodness you kept the mask on. You didn't swallow water, did you?"

"No, not much, only when I took the mask off."

"Mask off!" he said incredulously, "you took the mask off! I explained yesterday that you should never take it off in the water!"

"I had to, it began to leak when I laughed at a huge parrot fish."

"You are incredible, and I mean literally unbelievable. That has got to be the stupidest thing I ever heard. Laughing at a fish!"

"Don't scold me," she said plaintively, "please."

He took her hand again and turned it over, looking at it and her arms carefully in the light.

"Did you touch any of the coral, Sally? You must have. I warned you yesterday about fire coral. You have welts all over your arms. Does it itch?"

"Toward the end I had to pull myself along the ledge. I couldn't swim any more. I got tired. I wasn't worried about fire coral or anything else, just wanted to get to shore."

She closed her eyes against the memory of her struggle and snuggled into his arms, inhaling the scent of his body. He smelled of sea and sun and cleanliness and health. She felt safe with him. He tightened his arms around her and lightly kissed the top of her hair.

"Would you like to get up now, or do you want to rest a while longer?"

"I think that I would like to get up," she laughed aloud, "and take a nice hot bath."

"Why are you laughing?"

"It a private joke," Sally replied, teasingly, "between me and someone very dear to me."

His expression grew stern.

"Oh really?" He turned to go to the door. "I'll leave you then."

She asked, "Where's Teddy? Is he working?"

Brian's mouth tightened. "Yes, he has work to do down here, in case you have forgotten. Do as you like!" He walked out of the room and closed the door with deliberation.

She felt as though she had been doused with ice water.

Sally put her legs over the side of the bed, astounded by their weakness. Holding on to the walls, she stumbled to the bathroom. I will take a hot bath. What did he mean just now? Why does he change from being so warm and kind to acting as though I were untouchable? I said nothing to make him change. I can never trust him again. I wish that my unconscious self were as disciplined as I am. I won't have any thing to do with him. Every time I let myself go with him, he slaps me down. He must know how I feel about him. I know that I was so happy to have him find me. I remember the feeling of his carrying me in his arms down the beach. I wish that he would hold me that way again. But I can't allow myself to be vulnerable to him. For some reason he needs to hurt me. I don't know why. Tears, unbidden, fell into the tub.

She toweled herself dry and slipped into a bare-backed white cotton sun dress. Opening the door to the living room she found Mary on the couch.

"Well, you made a mess as usual. Ruined everyone's plans. You are a detriment to this organization. Somehow you always need to call attention to yourself. Theatrical, that's what you are. If you had lived in another time, you probably would have indulged in hysterical fainting so that everyone would worry about you. I was instructed to stay here until you showed yourself. Brian doesn't want anything to happen to anyone on this trip. Can you imagine the publicity, 'photographer's assistant drowns on Lassiter assignment.' That's all the store needs! You do need a Nanny, but if it were up to me, I would get one who believed in corporal punishment!"

Mary got up angrily, threw down the magazine she was reading and marched out the door.

Sally, literally recoiling from this attack, leaned against the wall.

Mary must be right about one thing. That was the reason for Brian's solicitude. He couldn't afford bad publicity! She had read what she wanted to read into his actions. It was just that she longed for him to care but he did not care for her at all. It was obvious that she was an object to him, just as most people were objects, to serve his needs or his ends. Mary and he were a good team! Yes, they deserved each other. They were both cold fish!

Resolving again to extirpate him from her heart, Sally threw open the patio door and walked down the beach to the ocean. Not again she thought. This time I'm just going to take a lounge chair and sit for the rest of the day. Ow, this itches. She looked at the welts on her arms caused by the fire coral. I guess if that's the worst of this morning's episode, I'm lucky. The shadows of the palm trees on the sand showed that it was late afternoon. I must have slept a good portion of the day away. I know that I went out before breakfast. No wonder I'm so hungry. I haven eaten anything all day. She looked down the beach to see if she could see one of the men who serve drinks. Raising her arm to signal, she winced. The welts were most uncomfortable, in addition to the fact that the arm felt like lead from the exertions of the morning.

She ordered a club sandwich and a tall glass of lemonade. sipped thirstily at the beverage when it arrived, and then leaned her head back against the chair staring out to sea.

I'm not helping Teddy, and he really doesn't need me. Impulsively she pushed herself out of the chair and hurried through the room and into the corridor leading to the lobby.

"When is the next flight out of here," she asked the woman at the travel desk.

She made arrangements for a taxi to pick her up. There was a plane leaving in an hour. How lucky, she thought, I can pack and get out before anyone is back. I hope that they don't get back early. I don't even know where they went today. She quickly threw her things together and called for a bellboy, and explained at the desk that she was only one of several people in the Presidential suite. Furtively she looked around as she waited for the desk clerk to take the message she addressed to Teddy, and ran to enter the taxi when it pulled up to the entrance. As it pulled away from the hotel she looked behind at the modern Mayan pyramid the hotel pretended to be. She sighed deeply. Resolutely she turned to face the front of the auto and made up her mind to find another job as soon as she got home.

She felt like a failure. All washed up at the age of twenty-three.

She laughed cheerlessly at herself. I messed up two jobs in the short time that I've been out of school. That's got to be a record for anyone! I have to check my balance at the bank as soon as I get home and see how much money I have. If I made enough working with Teddy, I think that I'll pull up stakes and move west. There's nothing to keep me there. Aunt Helen wants to go as well. Good riddance to Brian and Lassiter's and Mary. I hope I never see any of them again.

She got to the airport in plenty of time. I hope that they don't come back and find me gone before the plane leaves. I don't want Teddy coming down here and making a scene. In the note I explained that I just thought it would be better if I went home. I know that it won't be enough for him. He won't understand. Maybe he'll think that I was just upset about the swimming this morning. I hope that will be how he takes it. I know that Brian won't stop me. He will be glad to get me out of the way. I'm nothing but an annoyance to him. I hate Mary but she certainly is right about his worrying about his precious store. I am just an embarrassment to him.

She boarded the plane when the call came and walked sadly to her seat.

OTHER THAN A FEW POSTCARDS, Aunt Helen hadn't heard from Sally. She had hoped that it meant that Sally was having fun and hadn't the time to write. Indeed, she had no idea how long Sally and Teddy had planned to be away, as they had not even known themselves when they left.

It's such a good experience, she thought to herself. I hope that she's learning a lot. Aunt Helen had been looking through some government pamphlets on climate, and rainfall, humidity, population and all other things that might interest her in choosing a place to spend the rest of her life. She knew for sure that she was going to move out of this area and try something else better suited to her old bones, as she called them. Suddenly she was startled to hear the key click in the lock. Before she had time to react, the door was flung open and she heard her niece call her name.

Rushing to the entrance she embraced Sally.

"Darling, how are you? Did you have fun? Sit down and tell me all about it. Goodness, what's all over your arms! It looks like poison ivy. Sit down, sit down."

Sally tiredly pushed her suitcase into the room with her foot and said,

"Darling Aunt Helen, you know so much and I know so little. I am an absolute fool."

Aunt Helen stepped back open mouthed.

"What's wrong? I thought this would be such a wonderful adventure for you."

"Adventure, it was. Wonderful, it wasn't. I discovered things about myself and other people that I just don't like. Aunt Helen, I don't want to be in the city any more. Let's just pick up and get out of here. Have you decided where you want to go?"

"Sally," Aunt Helen said sternly. "You had better begin at the beginning and take me straight to the end. What happened to you? Why are you so outraged? Did someone hurt you? I want to know everything, and while you're at it you might as well include all of the problems that went before. You might just start when you began working at the store. It was so wonderful at the beginning. Start there and tell me everything."

Wistfully, Sally said,
"Do you have a week to listen?"
"You know that I have as long as it takes to hear the whole story. Start talking. I want to know why you want to run away."

Sally, sitting at the end of the couch with her feet tucked under her, looked like an unhappy little girl. Aunt Helen sat next to her holding her hand and listened. Sally started at the beginning with her first meeting of Brian and told Aunt Helen everything including her last encounter this morning with him. She had sense enough not to comment on her niece's foolhardiness and the dangerous things that she did. Instead she just held open her arms and hugged her and let the girl weep until she could cry no more. When Sally's sobs subsided she said, so quietly she could hardly he heard,
"I think that I dislike myself most of all. How could I be so stupid as to fall in love with an unfeeling ogre?"
"You must be very tired. I'll run you a tub and make a light supper for you and then we'll think about what to do. I think that it's a mistake to run away. You have to face down failures. As I see it, you haven't failed at your jobs. You have just made errors in judgment and allowed a man to interfere with your thinking. Be true to yourself, honey. You are the same wonderful person that you were before. You know that Hank cares for you, and from what you say Teddy does too. It can't be all your fault. Come on sweetheart, I'll fill the tub."

Sally smiled bitterly, thinking how Brian had bridled when she mentioned her secret friend who liked hot baths.
She discussed her future with Aunt Helen for days, batting back and forth the advantages of leaving the city and finding new horizons somewhere else or attacking her career here. But what is my career? I thought that it would be in retailing, and then I went into modeling and being a photographer's assistant. I don't really have a direction. Somehow I have been diverted. I ran away from the store because

of what happened with Brian. She blushed as she thought about her incomplete surrender to him that day. Often she had wondered what it would have been like had Hank not interrupted them. This was the only thing that she had not told Aunt Helen the truth about. In the expurgated version it had only been a passionate kiss in the beautiful garden. There had been no bedroom and no bed in that story. She still was embarrassed that she had let go so completely. As distressed as she was about Brian's attitude toward her, her unconscious would not abandon him. Her dreams, day and night, were tormented by his presence as much as they would have been if he were physically with her.

Aloud she said to Aunt Helen,

"What should I do?"

"I can't tell you that, Sarah, only you can make the decision. If you are sure that this man is as you describe him, cold and unfeeling, you would be better off to forget him. Go out and apply for a job with a photographer. You seem to like that. But you can't sit mooning around here. It is not good for you."

Fortunately, Teddy had given Sally copies of all her photographs from the gallery show. She contacted a few photographers whom she had gotten to know and got quite a bit of work. However, she found it boring and tiring. Without Teddy behind the cameras, there was no spirit or spark in the job. She knew now that she was a good model but understood that the captivating quality of those earlier photos was due to Teddy's genius. Much of the credit for the photography's success had to go to his quixotic poses and setups. His sense of humor came through all of his work. How I wish that I could love Teddy, she thought, but he's just not for me.

She spent several weeks in this desultory fashion. She had asked Aunt Helen to tell anyone who called that she was out of town. Her spirit and her heart were too sore to see either Teddy or Hank again. She did not want to be reminded of any part of the trip. She knew that she owed Teddy an explanation for her desertion, but she could not bring herself to call him. He had tried to contact her, but Aunt Helen had done as she asked.

"It isn't a lie," she defended her request. "I really am out of town, emotionally and mentally. I just don't want to talk to anybody. I have nothing to say yet. I'll call him when I do."

As depressed and unhappy as she was, she began losing weight again. Gone was the ravishing girl who had been so startling in Mexico. Her spark and vitality seemed to have been sapped. There was nothing that Aunt Helen could do to bring her out of her sadness.

In spite of herself, no matter how hard she tried she was unable to forget the feel of Brian's muscular arms around her. She relived over and over every episode in their fragmented relationship. She could not get out of her mind that strange whisper that came across the ball court in Chichen Itza. What does "I will not share her" mean? She was sure that it was a man's voice. But there were three men there. Could it have been Brian? But if it were, what could he have meant? Was he talking about Mary? Teddy was never that intense about anything. It couldn't have been he. That sound came from the bottom of someone's soul. But whose?

As time went on, she hoped that the emptiness in her heart would fill. When nothing seemed to work, she forced herself to galvanize.

The first thing I must do is to make amends with Teddy. I have to behave like a responsible adult, not a spoilt hurt child!

This decision alone made her feel better, so when she called him and he responded with,

"Of course, any time. You want your old job? We're a good team, princess. You should see the shots I got of you in Mexico. They are unbelievable. When do you want to come down to the studio?" He was so effusive in his welcome that she found it impossible to apologize for her behavior; he stopped her every time she tried.

"Say listen, babe, I knew that something was troubling you even there. Every once in awhile you'd be some place else. I would be talking to you and your mind would be a hundred miles away. Don't worry about it. Come on and get back to work. It will do you good. Don't be ashamed. It's not the first time my assistant has walked out on me."

Her days began to be interesting again as they began to pull together the campaign. Hank came down to the studio to work with them.

"How come you never answered my calls, Sally? Did I do something to offend you," he asked when the first uncomfortable minutes were over. They had circled each other like suspicious mutts for the first hour or so until they both had relaxed enough to see that neither would bite.

"No, Hank," he answered forthrightly. "I have been working through some of my own problems. I can't work at Lassiter's, but it has nothing to do with you. It's something that I have to resolve myself. I've behaved foolishly and immaturely. That's all I can say about it now. I'm sorry if I let you down, but I think that the campaign is good, and after all I did follow it up down there." She smiled, "I'm not all bad."

Seeing that there was nothing more to discuss, that Sally had closed the door on her feelings, he accepted it with a shrug and went on to talk to Teddy.

The photos had been sensational. Sally's original idea had been great. The advertising shots were exciting and eye-catching. A lot of the material was superimposed. It would have been a bit impractical to haul a microwave down to the beach, but the background shots did add the touch of surrealism as they had hoped.

"I'm very pleased with everything. You both did a great job. I'm going to bring them all in tomorrow for Lassiter to see them. He should be back by then."

"Back? Where is he? Didn't he come back with you, Teddy?" She turned to the photographer who was looking through a pile of pictures.

"Yep, he did, and a bloody bore he was too. Nasty and snappish. We flew back to Mérida and then took a commercial flight home from there. We got back a day or so after you, I think. But as pompous as he had before, you remember don't you Sal, how we made fun of him, he was just that much worse."

"Was he pleasant to Mary," asked Sally in a small voice.

"No different than to the rest of us. I tell you I was glad to get home. It wasn't as much fun after you left anyway. That was a dumb stunt you pulled incidentally."

"What did she do," asked Hank.

"Nearly got herself drowned to hear tell it, according to Lassiter. He claimed he found her on the beach half dead. You'd think that he was her father or something. It sounded like he wanted to spank her for being so dumb."

"You know, did you ever see a mother whose kid runs across the street it front of a car? When the kid is finally safe in her arms, she whacks it on the behind, she's so frightened and relieved at the same time. Well, that's the way he was with Sal. I thought that he would kill her, he was so mad at her."

"I know why," said Sally. "Mary told me why he was so mad."

"Mary is fairly reliable," said Hank. "She might have a good idea of what makes him tick. After all, she's been with him for years; she's a good girl."

"Well she may be up here, but down there she was the great stone face. Something was eating her all of the time. She was no joy to be with," said Teddy. "Anyway, Sal, what did she say?"

"She told me that if anything had happened to me, Brian would be furious because of the publicity."

"Publicity! What publicity?"

"She even quoted an imaginary headline to me, 'photographer's assistant drowns on Lassiter's assignment.'"

"Ah, she's just jealous," Hank said lightly, as he pawed through the photos.

"Teddy, these shots of Sally are terrific. They're amazing." He began to laugh. "What is this one? What are you wearing, a turban? And what's this, a life jacket? Look at Brian's face! I never saw him laugh like that. He's staring right at Sally."

"Let me see." Sally took the photos from him. Her heart liquified. Brian was looking at her as though he really cared for her. His blue eyes sparkled with joy, he looked so happy. She remembered the touch of her face on his cool stomach as she fastened the towel around his waist. She sighed deeply, as she also recalled her feeling that she had to move away from him or else she knew that she would melt as she had on that day in the Japanese garden, and then his sudden fury and accusations. Somehow he's always angry with me - but I don't know why.

She pulled herself back into the present and turning to Hank she said,

"How come you didn't come down? You were supposed to run the whole thing."

"It was Lassiter's idea. He said that he wanted to go for a few days to see how it was working out, and then he would come up and I would go down. He didn't want the store left without either one of us here. Well, then he called me and told me that he would see it through and that I had better stay at the store. I wondered why he changed his mind, but I just work here, he's the boss. I really envied you both, I wished I could have been with you."

"He's certainly a strong personality," said Teddy. "Nothing wishy-washy about him."

"He's not the easiest person to get along with," Hank said. "I would hate to get in his way if he really wanted something. Thankfully, he's never lost his temper with me. That's one thing I wouldn't like to see."

Sally turned on both of them angrily.

"Is there no other topic of conversation other than Brian Lassiter? He's a boor, a bore, mean and nasty. Can we finish with him now? I'm sick of the subject." She turned her back on both of them and walked over to the window. Teddy and Hank exchanged a look.

"Must be the weather that makes her irritable," teased Hank.

"It's true though, it's terribly muggy and the air is so still, feels like we're in for rain. I hope we get some," Teddy replied.

Hank said, "I'm going back to the store now. The shots are terrific. I'll call you tomorrow. Brian should be back by then, as I said. He just took off without telling anyone where. Mary is furious. I'll be in touch, so long."

He brushed Sally's cheek with his lips.

"You've lost weight since those pictures were taken."

"You know the cameras always put ten pounds on you," Sally said with a smile, trying to pass over her temper display.

"Bye, Hank."

"It's true, Sal, you have lost weight again. It's not the camera. You looked terrific in the Yucatan, but now you look so drawn. You ought to eat more," said Teddy.

Everybody has an answer Sally thought bitterly to herself. I'm the only one who knows what is wrong. I love a man who doesn't even like me and there's nothing I can do about it. I am trying to forget him, but it's like plucking out my own heart. I can't stop thinking about him.

Sally and Teddy worked throughout the rest of the afternoon, Teddy instructing her as to the cropping and laying out of the photos.

"It's getting dark very early," Teddy commented. "Looks as though there might be a storm coming up." Just as he said that a brilliant flash of light filled the room as a jagged streak of lightning illuminated the rapidly blackening sky. Almost instantaneously a deafening crash of thunder filled the small studio.

"Whew, that is hitting close," said Teddy.

"How can you tell?"

"The time that elapses between the flash of the lightning and the burst of thunder indicates how far away the lightning hit. You count the seconds between the flash and the boom.

"I didn't know that," said Sally.

"Lassiter isn't the only one who knows all kinds of things," teased Teddy. "I know one or two myself."

"I'm sure you do, Teddy," Sally said distractedly. "Listen to that rain pour down. I better close the window, the wind is blowing the pictures all over." She ran to the window and rapidly shut it.

"Teddy, you should see what's happening on the street."

The wind was tearing along the avenue, blowing people against the walls and turning umbrellas inside out.

"That's some squall! Put on the radio, will you, let's see if they have anything to say about this storm."

"...and this seems to be localized but there are similar storms all along the coast. Storm warnings have been issued for Long Island Sound and the Great South Bay. The near gale force winds are shortly expected to reduce their velocity but the small craft warnings are still in effect. There are flood warnings along Long Island parkways and the New Jersey highways. The storm should abate within a short while in the metropolitan area There...."

"Okay Sal, you can turn it off. That's better. It seems to be getting lighter even now. What a funny storm! It came in without warning and disappeared so quickly. Has it stopped raining now?"

Sally went over to the window. The sounds of the thunder were receding and the sky was becoming perceptibly lighter.

"Summer storms. I love thundershowers. They seem to clean the air," Teddy said offhandedly, deliberately not looking at Sally. "Sometimes it takes a good storm to clear the atmosphere."

Sally realizing that the comment meant more than it apparently did, but not wanting to pursue Teddy's train of thought, just mumbled,

"You're right, Teddy."

Teddy shook his head made a face, and decided not to continue with the conversation. They worked silently for a while until he said,

"I think that's enough for today, Sal, why don't you go home now, unless I could convince you to come to dinner with me."

"Thanks Ted, but I think another time. OK?"

"Whatever you say, lady, the rain's stopped now anyway."

Sally walked slowly home. Teddy was right about one thing. The air smelled fresh and clean. There was something magical about thundershowers. They did wash the air clean and make it fresh and sweet-smelling.

Aunt Helen had dinner ready when she got home. She had gone to the trouble of getting things that she knew Sally liked to eat. There was a fresh lobster and a dozen clams, boiled potatoes, and she had even made a flan, that custard covered with caramelized sugar that Sally had told her she had in Mexico.

Although she had walked all the way home, Sally was not particularly hungry, but when she realized the effort and the thought that had gone into the dinner, she made a valiant attempt to eat.

"It's really marvelous," Aunt Helen. "The flan is great. How did you find out how to make it?"

"Mrs. Mendez, who lives in Apartment 23C comes from Mexico, and I just went over to ask if she knew how to make it. Her husband works at the Mexican Embassy and I thought that she could give me an authentic recipe. As a matter of fact, she told me how to make the lemon soup that you had liked so well. I'm going to try that next."

Sally got up from the table to give her a hug. "There's no one sweeter than you."

"That may be true, but I don't seem to do you much good, Honey."

"Aunt Helen, the time for anyone to help me is over. I have to work through the problems, most of which I have created, myself. I simply have to get over this feeling for a man who doesn't know whether I am alive or dead, nor does he care."

"I'm glad to see that you have started work again. It's the best thing for you."

"It is, I agree, but today was hard because we were looking at pictures of the trip, and I kept being reminded of Brian and all of the unpleasant and pleasant things that happened."

"I know darling, but that's part of the cure too. You have to face the past and try to look at it objectively so that you can put it into perspective. The things that embarrassed you and that seem so horrendous will diminish in importance with time, and eventually Brian, too, will become part of the past without the emotion that goes with him now."

Sally picking up the dishes to bring them into the kitchen said,

"I know, I'm trying.It will be better when Teddy and I start on a different project so that I don't have to be constantly reminded of the trip."

She turned the water on at the sink, preparing to rinse the dishes before putting them into the machine.

"I wish...," she was interrupted by the ringing of the phone.

Aunt Helen picked up the instrument, stilling it's insistent sound.

"Hello, oh yes, Teddy, how are you? Sure she's right here."

Sally dried her hands on her apron and took the phone.

"Hi, Ted....OK, I'll get a chair, why....My God, when, where is he?"

Slowly she rested the phone back on its cradle, her face ashen.

"Sally, what's wrong?" Aunt Helen walked over to the slumped girl.

She looked up into Aunt Helen's face and slowly said, there's been an accident."

"Who? Whom are you talking about, Sally? She shook her impatiently. "Sally answer me."

"It's Brian. Ted said that Brian had been in an accident."

"Where is he? Did he tell you how it happened?"

"No, he was at Hank's house. Mary had called Hank and told him. She was going out there."

"Out where? Where is 'there'?"

"I don't know, Aunt Helen. I don't know anything. I don't even know what happened, and there's no one that I can ask except Hank. I certainly can't call Mary. She's probably left already and she would just tell me it's none of my business."

"Why don't you try calling the store?"

"It will be closed by now. And they probably don't know anything anyway. What can I do?"

She ran to Aunt Helen and threw her arms around her. Helen patted her on the head the way she had done when she was a small child needing comfort.

"There's nothing that you can do, baby, nothing at all. We will just have to see what information we can get tomorrow. Maybe

Hank will know more then. You can call him in the morning after he gets to the office. Did Teddy say what he was going to do tonight?"

"No," he hung up after he told me the news. "He said that he didn't know what to do either."

"Why don't you try calling Hank at home in a little while. Maybe he will have learned something by then. Did Teddy say where Hank was going?"

"No, he said he was leaving, but he didn't say where he was going."

"Try calling him at home in an hour. Maybe he will know something by then."

Sally called Hank every hour on the hour that night, but there was no answer. She tried to find a telephone number for Brian in the directory, but there was nothing.

Even though Aunt Helen gave her some hot milk with a little brandy in it she tossed all night.

Her impotency was what enraged her so. There was nothing that she could do. She didn't even have any information about the accident, if it were an accident. Her dreams, when she did manage to fall asleep, were tormented and woke her up. Activity, any activity was better than lying there. She tried to read but couldn't keep her thoughts on what she was reading. Aloud she said to herself,

"I'll call Hank as soon as it gets light."

She paced her bedroom back and forth. Fearful of waking her aunt, she tiptoed into the kitchen to make some tea. Looking at the clock, and sure that it was almost morning, she was shocked to discover that it was only 2:30. I'll never survive this night, she thought. I don't even know if he's alive or dead. Even if he makes fun of me, and I know that he will, I want to tell him that I love him before he dies. DIES! The thought of forceful Brian not alive shattered her. It is not possible for such a vital man to be dead. I know that he is not! She felt that her will was enough to keep him alive. Even if Mary is there, I'll tell him there is no one else I can ever love. I don't care if she is her usual sarcastic self. Nothing matters any more. She drank the tea as slowly as she could, thinking at least an hour had passed only to discover that the hands had advanced only fifteen minutes. I know that he won't care, but I have to tell him anyway. Again she looked at the clock, it had barely moved. She picked up her cup and walked back to the bedroom. She drank the rest slowly and lay down again on the bed. Finally she got up again and moving a chair over, sat at the window watching the desolate street. She fell asleep with her head on the sill where Aunt Helen found her the next morning at seven o'clock. She started out of her sleep as she heard her aunt's footsteps. She knew immediately where she was and what she had to do.

"I'm going to call Hank. Maybe I can reach him at home." She rushed to the phone and dialed Hank's number. The phone rang and rang hollowly. There was no answer. Sorrowfully she replaced it in the cradle and walked over to the stove. Slowly and deliberately she measured out coffee and in the same controlled manner filled the pot with four cups of water. She opened the refrigerator and chose four oranges and carefully squeezed them. It was though, by her deliberate movements, she were able to control her thoughts.

Aunt Helen walked into the kitchen.

"Here, darling, this is today's paper. I thought that we might find out something in here." She held out the folded paper to Sally who grabbed it out of her hand.

She quickly scanned the front page, but there was nothing about Brian Lassiter mentioned.

"He's not famous enough to be on the front pages, look further back."

She walked behind the girl and leaned over her shoulder. Together they tore through the paper.

"Nothing. There's nothing here."

"Get dressed Sal. Pull yourself together. We'll try the store in a little while."

"No," said Sally. "I'm not going to call. I am going over there. If Mary's back I may have to face her - well, then I'll just have to face her. Somehow I'll get the information."

"Do you want me to go with you, honey?"

Sally drew herself up tall as she could.

"No, Aunt Helen, I have to start taking charge of my own life. I'll do it alone. I have plenty of time for another cup of coffee, and by then I can dress and leave."

She forced herself to sit down and become calm. She felt a numbness descend. She knew now that she would be able to handle any situation that arose. She could even handle not knowing what had happened because she was sufficiently in control of herself to find out.

Before she left she tried Hank one more time, but there still was no answer. She walked all the way to the store. Deliberately she put one foot in front of the other. The only way that I can manage this is to do just that. If I take one step at a time I will be able to be in control of the situation.

The store looked exactly the same as it had that first day she had applied for the executive training job. How long ago that seemed. How free and happy I was then. How excited I had been about getting the job. She sighed deeply, and walked to the back elevator. She pushed the button to the Administrative Office. Noticing again that funny keyhole on the top of the row of buttons, her loins felt like liquid as she remembered the day she had almost succumbed. Now that she didn't know what had happened to Brian, her feeling was no longer of shame that she had let herself go so far, but rather sorrow that they had not been able to consummate their love. For she preferred to think that at that time and on that day in that place, Brian had loved her as much as she had loved him. She remembered only the good and beautiful things about him. The touch of his hand when he picked up her overturned purse, the depths of his kiss in the park, the feel of the power in his arms as he carried her along the beach. I must see him alive again, she thought fiercely to herself. I must!

The elevator finally reached the Administration floor. She walked over to the receptionist's desk. There was no one there. She turned down the corridor to Hank's office and flung open the door. Hank was stretched out on the couch. She ran over to him and shook him roughly.

"Hank, Hank, wake up, what has happened to Brian?"

"Sally! What are you doing here? Brian is hurt. How did you find out? Why did you come?"

"Stop asking me questions, Hank. Tell me what happened."

Hank struggled to sit up.

"I've been here ever since the news came in yesterday. I was afraid to leave the phone. He's been hurt very badly, Sally, they are not sure that he's going to live. He's in a coma. But why do you care? I got the impression from Teddy that you didn't like him very much. He said that you and he fought constantly."

Sally ignored his questions.

"Where is he, Hank? I've got to go to him."

Hank shook his head incredulously.

"I don't understand but...He's out on Long Island. He was out at his place. He has this mansion on an island in the Sound, you know, and he was taking the boat out there when apparently there was a freak gust of wind. You remember what the weather was like yesterday." She nodded.

"Well, apparently the boat was turned over in the storm. He hit his head and they pulled him out, unconscious. Fortunately, the custodian at his place was keeping tabs on him so that he was still down at the dock and he was able to get to the boat and pull him out before he drowned."

"Where is he now?"

"They were waiting for daylight and then they are going to bring him into the city by helicopter. The hospital out there doesn't have the best facilities "

"Is he alone?"

"Of course not, he has the best medical care that anyone can buy. A doctor and a nurse flew out to pick him up."

"I don't mean that. I mean is any of his family with him."

"No, he doesn't have anybody. Mary drove out last night so that she could be with him. She's about the closest person he has. She's been with him the longest of anyone. He's really a loner, doesn't have any close friends either. Just me, I guess, and I'm really not a bosom buddy, you might say."

"When can I see him?"

"YOU, why? You didn't answer me before. What is he to you?"

Sally didn't answer him, she just stared at him, her eyes huge with hurt and fear.

Suddenly it dawned on Hank.

"You're in love with him," he whispered incredulously.

"You poor kid, he'll never give you the time of day. He swore that he would never become involved with any woman. The store is his life. Poor Mary has been trying to get him for years, I suspect."

"Hank," she whispered intensely. "I have to see him. Arrange it please."

Hank stared solemnly at her. He held her hand tightly. "I wish it could have been me, Sal. Maybe it will be one day. But he's not for you even if he lives. He needs no one, and he wants no one. Right now they don't even know if he'll live. But, hell, I would do anything you asked."

He called the hospital to which Brian was being transferred.

"They don't know anything there yet. Come on, it will be easier if we just go down there and wait. Maybe we'll get some information if we are on the spot."

Gratefully, Sally kissed his cheek.

"I can't tell you all about it now. You may be right. He probably doesn't love me. Sometimes I think he cares about me, and other times I think that he doesn't know I'm alive, or worse, actually dislikes me. But I have to see him for myself. I have to tell him what I feel, even if I am hurt by doing so. I have to face reality and this is the first step."

"You certainly sound calm and collected. You sound as though you have thought everything out."

"I've tried to ever since I heard about the accident. I have to take charge of my life again. I have to learn to see the world as it is, not as I want it to be. If he dies, that's a truth that I would have to face. If he lives and tells me that he doesn't want any part of me, that too is something that I have to handle. If..." She stopped embarrassedly.

Hank finished for her, "If he loves you, and tells you so...Ah Sally, that's a dream. It will never happen."

"Maybe so," she bridled, "but I have to know it. I have to hear it from him."

"Well, old girl, I'll be there to help to pick up the pieces. For your sake and the store's welfare, I hope that he lives. Come on, let's get over to the hospital."

I must have walked twenty-five miles, Sally muttered to herself. She had covered the corridor so many times that she was sure that she had permanently etched her path in the gleaming white vinyl floor. She was only vaguely aware of the activity that went on in that hall. The nurse's station had a battery of screens with lines and pulsations appearing on them. She understood that they were the monitors connected with the patients in the rooms behind the ominously closed doors. Finally Hank appeared, a broad grin in evidence. He grabbed her and hugged her tightly.

"He's going to be all right."

"Can I see him, is he awake, conscious?"

"Yes, he's not too bad considering that it was a bad blow, and the water that he swallowed before he was pulled out didn't help at all. It really wasn't necessary to bring him all the way back here. But the Lassiter name in that small community frightened them. They felt they weren't capable, and didn't want to take the responsibility of his care. Everything was exaggerated - But he won't be out of here so fast - they need to keep him under observation."

She jiggled is arm.

"Can I see him, did you see him?"

118

"Yes, I saw him but I don't know if you can."
Furiously, she said,
"Why not?"
"Well, Sally what do I tell them? I at least am his assistant. I work for him. I'm his number 1 man. There was a rationale, but what do I say about you? Wife? Obviously not, sister, a lie, fiancée, not so. What are you, if anything, to him?"
She flushed with anger and frustration. What was she to him?
"A friend. Can't you say that I'm a friend?"
"I guess so, but I don't know when they are going to let 'just friends' see him. A doctor passed them as they stood arguing. Hank addressed him,
"This young lady would like to see Mr. Lassiter. Would it be possible?"
Observing Sally carefully, the doctor saw the carelessly dressed hair, pulled back with loose tendrils around her face, lack of make-up and purple rings under the eyes. In spite of the disarray of her appearance, he was aware of her beauty. Her lack of concern for her grooming indicated the depths of her worry. Meeting her imploring eyes he realized that Lassiter must mean a great deal to her. Assuming that she was of equal importance to him he said, in answer to her mute appeal,
"I think that he's going to be all right. I'll leave instructions for you to be able to see him tomorrow. But he's resting now. He's asleep." He put his arm on hers. "You can wait 'till tomorrow. Nothing will happen between now and then. The best thing for you to do is to get some rest. Did you sleep last night?" She shook her head negatively.
"I thought not. Then go home now and go to bed. We'll watch over him. Don't worry." He patted her arm. "Tomorrow," he said as he walked away. "I'll leave word for you to see him tomorrow. Tell them your name at the desk as you go out."
"OK, Sally." Hank took her by the elbow and turned her in the direction of the elevator. "Go home. You can't give him your famous message today. It will just have to wait and so will you. Let's go. I'll get you a cab and then I am going to the office."

Instead of going home, Sally went to work. Teddy had a very silent assistant that day. She spoke hardly at all. She was relieved that Brian was going to be all right, but confessing her love became more and more difficult to contemplate. It was easy when there was a high bedside drama in mind. But now that she knew he wasn't going to die, she wondered if she would have the nerve to tell him her secret. True to her new resolve of facing life truthfully, she said to herself, the most I can do is try, and try I must.

The next day Sally went to the hospital and presented herself at the nurse's station.

"The doctor told me that I was going to be able to see Mr. Lassiter today. May I go in now," she asked the young nurse who was seated at the station.

"Why yes, he only has one visitor now. You may go in," she said after she consulted her computer.

The nurse, had been smitten by Brian's good looks. She was the one who had given him his morning bath and had been treated to a flash of his brilliant smile. What a handsome couple this girl and he would make she thought begrudgingly. Some women have all the luck.

Even before Sally reached his door she heard the icy tones with which he was scathing some poor soul. Sally smiled to herself in happiness to hear those familiar sounds. That must be a good sign; he sounds almost normal. I wonder whom he is scolding. She knocked lightly at the door.

A woman's voice responded,

"Come in." It was Mary.

Sally wanted to turn and run. Of all the people in this world, Mary was certainly the last one whom she wanted to see. Throwing her head back and squaring her shoulders, she resolved to go through with it. She pushed the door open. Brian's back was toward her; he was facing the window and was not interested enough to turn around until Mary said,

"What are YOU doing here?"

At that Brian turned toward the door. Seeing his beloved face, with the white bandage around his head, Sally didn't care that Mary was there. Indeed, she forgot her presence completely. She ran over to the bed and reached out her arms to him and was rewarded by a luminous smile. His blue eyes shone with the same love that she remembered from that first day in the park.

"Don't touch him! Are you mad? He's badly injured. You shouldn't be here anyway. Who allowed you in?"

Mary had rapidly come to the foot of the bed and was about to push Sally away.

"STOP!"

It obviously was a strain on Brian to emit such a bellow. Horrified at what it might do to his condition, Sally turned on her heel and fled the room, Mary at her heels. She grabbed her by the shoulders and shook her, causing Sally's hairpins to fly out and her hair to tumble down her back.

"What is this?" The deep tones of the physician with whom Sally had spoken yesterday stopped Mary from continuing her attack.

"This is a hospital, Miss," he addressed her. "There are sick people in here including the gentleman in that room. Your lack of control is regrettable. If you don't take yourself in hand, I am afraid that you will have to leave."

"I am Mr. Lassiter's secretary. It is imperative that I have free access to him. This woman," she pointed angrily, "is nothing to him; he doesn't even like her. She has done him harm in the past and I think that she should not be allowed to see him when he is in a weakened condition."

Mary trembled with righteous indignation as she unleashed this tirade.

Sally stood her ground, saying nothing until the ill-tempered woman had finished. Then, addressing the doctor she said quietly and with dignity,

"There is nothing that I would do to harm Mr. Lassiter. If my visit would in truth harm him, I certainly would leave immediately.... but," her eyes filled with tears. Impatiently wiping them away, she continued, "I will do whatever you say."

The doctor remembering the pain in those deep brown eyes yesterday as she begged to see Brian, said to Mary,

"You calm down or I will have to ask YOU to leave the premises." To Sally, he said,

"What is your name? I will take this up with the gentleman in question. Both of you stay out of the room now. I have to examine him now."

"Sally, my name is Sally Harte."

She walked away from Mary to the end of the corridor where she stared out of the window, looking down at the street far below, not seeing anything except the expression of warmth in those haunting blue eyes.

It seemed to be an interminable wait until the doctor came down the hall and tapped her on the shoulder.

"I have spoken to Mr. Lassiter. He would like very much to see you, but I don't want you to be in there for very long."

"How is he? Will he be all right," she looked at him imploringly. He answered as they walked back to Brian's room.

"I think that there won't be complications. As far as we can see, there has been no permanent damage. There will have to be further tests, but not today. We have been observing him very closely. It was a serious accident and could have been fatal. That he was pulled out so quickly was the only thing that saved him. As he had been knocked unconscious, he would have drowned. He owes a great debt to the fellow who was waiting for him at the dock in that terrible weather."

"I can see that you are impatient to get in there, no more than five minutes today." He smiled. "I'll make sure that spitting cat doesn't go in with you."

Sally pushed the door open. Brian was lying with his eyes closed. It was the first time that she had seen him when he was not awake. How handsome he is, she thought, even without the impact of those startlingly blue eyes. His face looked more gentle, he seemed so peaceful.

"I must have dozed off, but I smelled your presence. No one perfumes the air the way you do." He opened his eyes and lifted his hand languidly. She reached to take it gently and held it tightly in hers.

"Oh, Brian," she whispered. Then she bent down to kiss his hand, wanting to taste his lips but afraid. He softly touched her hair with his other hand.

"Sometimes you're such a good girl, Sarah. Like the nursery child, 'when she was good she was very, very good, but when she was bad she was horrid,' and you do have a curl in the middle of your forehead." He continued softly, "as I told you many times, you need a keeper."

"I think that you were the one to need a keeper the other day. I've never got myself into such serious trouble. What were you doing going out in that storm."

"I had to get away... Who told you about it?"

"Teddy, and then I spoke to Hank."

"Oh yes, your two pals." He pulled his hand back. "It was nice of you to come to see me. Thank you," he said abruptly.

"But Brian," the words that she had wanted to say and that she had thought would be so easy, when he had looked at her longingly, now seemed impossible. His eyes had become glacial. Those burning inviting eyes had become cold as ice.

He turned his head away.

"Good-by, I'm tired. Thank you for coming," he repeated formally.

Dismissed! She had been dismissed. She sadly walked toward the door.

"T EDDY, I'M TIRED OF THIS passive role. I don't want to be a model, I want to learn how to take photographs. That's the creative end, and it's much more interesting. Would you teach me?

"What do you think that you've been learning all this time. All that you need to do is try it. Here take a camera. Go. Go out and spend the day in the city. Take everything that appeals to you. When you get back, we'll develop them and see what you've gotten on film. Go!"

Teddy was happy to see Sally evidence an interest in anything. So she marched out that fall morning dressed in blue jeans and a bright green turtle neck pull-over sweater. With her camera and exposure meter slung over around her neck, she looked the part of a busy professional young New Yorker. She wandered out from the studio, trying to emulate Teddy in the way that he was able to envision a picture. After a while she stopped thinking about the way he would do it and began taking shots of things that interested her. All along elegant Fifth Avenue there were young people performing. A young flutist played Vivaldi at the bottom of a church's steps, her open flute case mutely inviting contributions. At another entrance, there a crowd gathered to watch a magician as entranced by the rabbits that he pulled out of his hat as they would have been had he been on a legitimate stage.

The fall air sparked with clarity. Summer had vitiated itself. The summer storms had spent themselves and New York was alive with the injection of cool air. It was time for a new beginning. Fall should be the beginning of the new year, not January she felt. It's time for a new beginning for me as well. She had been thinking of Brian less and less, although when she did the hurt of that bedside meeting went deep. I wish I knew, she pondered for the hundredth time, why he can be so loving one minute and so hateful the next. Is it anything

124

that I do that causes it? Impatiently she shrugged away the thought, and focused her attention on a young child seated on his father's shoulders. He was high enough to see over the crowd's heads and was squealing with delight and pointed at the rabbits coming out of the magician's hat. She aimed the camera at the little boy and took shot after shot of his gestures and wonderment.

"I'd like one like that," she said aloud, shocking herself. I've never thought about having a child before, but yes, I would like one like that". The father was enjoying the show as much as the little boy, and even when the baby grabbed on to his hair causing him to wince, his reprimand was so full of love that Sally wished she could be part of such a scene.

She wandered her way uptown until she reached the park. I know the best place would be the zoo. There are hundreds of kids and if that isn't enough, there are all of the animals.

Suddenly she realized that she was hungry. The smell of the hot dog vendor's wares had triggered her appetite. She ordered a hot dog with mustard and sauerkraut. There's nothing like a sidewalk New York hot dog she thought, as the mustard oozed out of the bun. Impatiently she licked her mouth. She was having trouble managing the food, her cameras and a napkin all at once.

"As always, you need a keeper!" The deep voice turned her loins to liquid.

She flushed as she wiped her face.

"Allow me!" Brian whipped a fragrant handkerchief out of his pocket, then soberly and gently wiped the corners of her mouth, holding her firmly by the back of her head as she tried to pull away.

"How dare you attack me like that?"

"Attack you? Hardly, my dear girl. I was just trying to clean you up. No matter how hard I've tried to teach you table manners, you never seem to learn." His eyes twinkled and crinkled at the corners as he flashed a bright teasing smile.

His navy blue blazer with a light blue turtle neck sweater heightened the color of his eyes.

"I can't say that you are the picture of high fashion, Sarah-Sally. What are you up to now? Is Teddy letting you out alone? How foolhardy!"

Suddenly remembering the grave danger that he had been in, her anger subsided as quickly as it had risen by his taunting words.

"Brian, why are you so mean to me? I'm so glad to see you. You look wonderful. Are you all right, really all right?" Anxiety and love flowed from her eyes.

He gazed down at her. "What's happened to you, Sally, that's the first time that you have talked to me as though I might be a friend, not as though I were an enemy?

"I?" She raised her voice, "I", she repeated. "You have never in your life said anything nice to me."

"Your memory is quite short. I seem to remember a day in the park...and another on a terrace."

She blushed, bringing color to her tanned cheeks.

"Yes, you did then. But you acted as though you hated me after that, and I felt ashamed to have loved you."

He took her by the elbow.

"I have had enough of this street scene. I want to talk to you if you think that we could have a civilized conversation. Do you? Are you capable of talking and not losing your temper?"

Oh, she thought. I don't believe that this conversation is happening. Oh, please, it's not I who loses my temper.

"I don't lose my temper. It's always you. You who turns cold without warning. I don't know what to make of you."

They were walking toward the store. At the entrance, Sally balked. "Oh no, no way will I go where that she-cat is. She's going to tear my eyes out, and I don't know why either. I never did anything to hurt her."

Brian laughed.

"I'll protect you from the tigress. Don't worry. Anyway, we're not going anywhere where she is."

He pushed her back toward the back elevator and after the last person had gotten off, he pulled out his key and fitted it into the lock on top of the buttons.

The elevator stopped at the exquisite little foyer. Brian pushed the door to the apartment. Leading her gently over to the garden, he opened the door and took her outside.

"I want to talk to you and this is one of the two best places in the world."

Unresistingly Sally let him turn her to him. He lifted her chin.

"Damn," he roughly pulled the cameras off her neck, and set them down. "Always a reminder of someone else."

Sally astounded again at this display of temper, this time said,

"What are you talking about Brian?" There had to be an answer to his mysterious behavior.

"Talk to me," she fairly shouted. "Every time you're kind and loving, something sets you off. What is it? Why do we end up fighting all the time and hurting each other?"

With great control, Brian said,

"Sally, I will not share you with another man. Evidently one man is not enough for you. First it was Hank and now it is Teddy."

Rigidly, unbelievingly Sally heard these words. "I will not share you" echoing over and over in her head just as they had at the ball court.

They were standing, each one tense and angry, apart from one another.

As much as it pained her to remind him of Mary, she said,

"What am I to make of that harridan, that cool, collected, murderous, impeccably groomed, proper Mary."

He laughed coldly.

"Have you run out of adjectives? She's a very good nurse as well as a secretary. She's been with me for years."

"I know that. Do you love her?"

"Love who? Love Mary? Why no," he said soberly.

"But you've slept with her," she accused him. "You've had an affair with her."

"Whether I have or not is really not your business, Sally. I am not a boy just out of school."

"What is that supposed to mean? That I am just out of school?"

"No, it's just supposed to mean that I don't see that it's any of your business."

"What is supposed to be my business? You talk about sharing me. You don't know what you are talking about. Besides, it's not any of your business either. You don't know if I even love you."

"Do you?" questioned Brian softly, and he held his breath.

Unable to resist him any longer, her anger dissolved.

For an answer she threw herself into his arms. He held her tightly, lifted her chin and pressed his mouth to hers. Throwing her arms around him she held him to her yearning body. As one they walked to the door leading to the beautiful bedroom overlooking the serene Japanese garden.

"No more words." He put his fingers on her lips. "Say nothing, we always spoil things by talking too much. We'll sort it out later, my darling."

Carefully he pulled the sweater over her head as she was seated at the edge of the bed. He gasped as he looked at the perfection of her body. Her rosy nipples emphasized the beauty of her full rounded breasts. He undressed her lower body and gazed at the magnificence of her offering. Quickly he tore off his own clothes and lay beside her.

"My darling, we will have the most beautiful children in the world." Then loosening her hair he buried his face in its fragrant depths.

Slowly, tantalizing he brought his lips to her mouth and their tongues made love. He withdrew and traced the map of her body with his lips and tongue until there was no place unexplored. Then gently, ever so gently he entered her. As his manhood met the resistance of a maiden he was startled and breathed aloud.

"I could never have dreamed that there has been no one. I have been wrong."

Sally, almost lost in another world, returned caress for caress, and when he entered her arched her back to meet him, returning his passion in kind.

As they lay in the deep big bed, nestled into one another's body, Brian said,

"Is next week too soon?"

There was no need for Sally to ask for what it might be too soon.

"Today, if you like, my only love, my darling."

"We have to take care of some practical matters, sweet child, like licenses, wedding plans. Impetuous as ever. You finally will have a keeper. I will take care of you forever," he whispered into her ear.

Sally and Brian had gone out to the island the next day. Like a little boy he wanted to show off all of his treasures to his bride-to-be.

When she met the man who had saved Brian that fateful stormy day, she impulsively embraced him.

"You saved my life too."

Initially Brian bristled at that physical contact, but he realized that his lady was always going to express herself physically.

"Not that she lacks the ability to express herself verbally either," he muttered to himself.

They had made such an effort to stop being jealous of others that Brian had never really gotten an explanation from Sally of her relationship to Teddy and Hank. He was just beginning to understand that her youthful exuberance included all of those people of whom she was fond. Touching was part of Sally. He had come to realize that the unplumbed depths of her passion had been untouched, unreleased until he had unlocked the gate. He knew now that she was his forever. It was with some reluctance, however, that he had agreed that she would continue working with Teddy.

They had been sitting on the large porch overlooking the Sound. She was curled up in a large wicker chair.

"I have to talk to you very seriously, Brian. I would like to spend some time perfecting my photography. I enjoy it and Teddy says that I have a good eye. He liked the shots that I showed him."

"You can take all of the pictures you want of our children," he said shortly.

"That's not enough! I need to do something on my own as well. I do want kids but I think that I would like to wait a little while. I want to work with Teddy too, so that I can get a good foundation. Then later I can continue to work on my own. That way I can be at home with the children and be involved with my own work at the same time."

She got out of the chair to come over to sit on his lap.

"I want to have you alone for myself for a few years anyway."

He held her tightly and said,

"That's the best proposition I have ever heard."

The wedding was a very simple affair. Both of them wanted it that way. The only guests were Teddy, Hank, Aunt Helen, Joan, Sally's brother and his wife, and all of Brian's servants. Mary had been invited, after Sally had become convinced that she had never meant anything to Brian. However, she had declined on the basis of her needing time to pack to move to Florida.

Brian was gracious and charming to Hank and Teddy. It was with a great deal of pleasure that he shook hands. All suspicion was gone as he finally realized that they had never been more than good friends to Sally. He understood now her effusiveness and knew that it was no more than a measure of her warmth.

She had looked magnificent as she descended the broad staircase. Her red hair had been dressed in a coronet braided with daisies. Her short princess gown was of white eyelet cotton, emphasizing the lines of her graceful figure. Her face was so radiant that all make-up was unnecessary.

As the last of the guests were taken back to the mainland, Brian and Sally climbed the golden oak staircase. As they paused to look out the window on the landing, Sally pulled Brian down to the seat with her.

"There's one thing that I could never understand. Did you know that I was Sally right away when we met in Mexico City?"

"No. You look so different with make-up that I really hadn't recognized you. It was only when you began to laugh so hard at the table that I realized that that obstreperous young applicant Hank was interviewing in his office, the girl in the park, the woman in my apartment, the minx in the photo gallery and you were one and the same."

"We've wasted so much time in misunderstandings," she said.

"We have a lifetime to make it up," he answered. "Would you like to start now?"

He pulled her gently to her feet and led her up the stairs.

About the Author

Having traveled widely, Ms Starr spices her romances with her own worldly experiences. She brings to her writing the excitements of her own varied life. She and her heroines firmly believe that they can overcome adversity with humor, courage daring and a large dose of self-confidence.